Home Familiar Home

Accidental Familiar 4

Belinda White

Authors Note:

I wanted to forewarn you that this book references a character and story that you might not have seen yet. Giovanni Rosati and his history with Amie and her crew is currently a side project that I am writing with my newsletter peeps.

We're having a whole lot of fun with it! If you want to be a part of that, you can join my newsletter and help us to build a better story.

Once it's complete, the whole world can see it. For now, it's just for us. But don't worry, that won't detract from this book at all. I simply didn't want you all to think you'd missed something!

Happy reading.

Chapter 1

"My turn, my turn!" Mason yelled. Unfortunately, he was right outside my bedroom door when he did.

The kids had invented a new game—something they'd seen on the internet, I think. It involved a long sturdy piece of cardboard and a quick and speedy trip riding it down the farmhouse stairs.

I'll admit, it looked like fun. But it was a loud and very noisy endeavor. Add that to the sounds of a newborn demanding to be fed at all hours of the night, and you pretty much have my life right now.

Not that I'm complaining. I love my new extended family and friends.

Mason and his mom had come into our lives a few weeks ago. Right before she gave birth to little baby Pearl. I think that might have been what sealed the deal on them living here for longer than Opal had originally planned.

Kimberly was really smart to give her baby girl the same name as my grandmother. Then again, seeing Aunt Opal with the children, it might not have made all that much of a difference after all.

Personally, I'm glad we can be there for them. They need us. I just really like school and work hours through the week, when I have the place all to myself.

Weekends like this were rough.

Even more so, as I didn't have Ruby to complain to. She was spending far more time at Arc's than here nowadays. Not that I blamed her. Opie's little apartment was looking mighty good right now too. But we weren't far enough along in our new friends with benefits type of relationship for me to spend that many nights there.

Arc and Ruby had raced ahead of us on that one.

I laid there and listened as the kids took turns down the bumpy homemade slide outside my room. At least they sounded like they were having fun. And I should be getting up and moving, anyway. I'd read about a new bond jumper in the paper, and my bank account was getting kind of low. Time to visit Boswell Bonds.

After a few stretches and a quick trip to the bathroom, I decided to start off by waking up right. Thanks to Opie, I'd been reintroduced to martial arts. Something I'd been missing out on for years. In that time frame, what with the aging in between and all, I'd lost some of my flexibility.

I had to work on that if I wanted to advance. After beating Missy in that unsanctioned cage fight, I knew she'd be itching for a rematch. I'd be more than happy to give it to her, but I wanted to be ready. I'd played a little dirty last time. Letting her take me down three times with pretty much no resistance while I learned her moves before I struck her down hard.

I'd won hands down. A fact that was driving the new sheriff's deputy more than a little crazy.

And yes, it still made me smile to think about it. I'm allowed to be petty sometimes, too.

A Tia Chi workout might not look all that strenuous, but if you do it right, it can be. Within half an hour I was feeling the burn. In a good 'I could so take over the world right now' kind of way.

That's when my phone rang.

"Hey, Ruby, glad to see you remembered my number."

"Ha-ha. I just saw you yesterday."

That was true, but I really wasn't going to count a quick dart into her old apartment across the hall to pick up more clothes as a true visit. I missed her, dash it all. She'd been a part of my everyday life for… well, all of my life up until now. The new normal was taking some major getting used to.

"For all of what? Two minutes?"

She laughed. "You're right. Doesn't count, does it? So, how about you join me and Arc for lunch at the chicken buffet place? Our treat. Then you can spend the afternoon with us." She paused. "There's something we want to show you."

I hesitated. I really wanted some time with Ruby alone, like the old days of a few months ago. But then again, how could I complain about getting quality time in with my new to me half-brother too?

We planned to meet in a half hour. Sue me, but I'd tried to have a sleep-in morning. It was quickly approaching noon. A quick shower later, and I was on the road.

I was happy enough at the prospect of spending some time with my cousin that I never even thought about the fact that she might have a hidden agenda.

I should have known better. After all, it was Ruby.

***

Clucky's Palace hadn't really changed all that much since the first time Opie and I had tried it out.

Well, except for their prices. For that much money, if it were up to me, I'd be heading to Carney's Pizza. But if they were buying, then a chicken buffet made a nice change in my diet. Probably a far healthier one too.

Even as quick as I'd been, they beat me there. Good thing, as the place was packed, and they had managed to get a table before the waiting list started.

The hostess led me over to their table, and Arc even got up to pull out my chair for me. That was my first real clue that something was up.

He wasn't normally that chivalrous when it came to his sister. Namely, me. The call from out of the blue after days of basically ignoring my existence in their newfound love life, the free dinner, and now an uncharacteristically nice brother? Oh yeah, something was most definitely up.

But hey, I was getting free food and time with two of my most favorite people on earth, so what was the harm in that? And with my track record, whatever it was they wanted, I'd most likely be more than willing to give it to them. Although, them pulling out all the stops like this did have me just a bit worried.

They had waited for me before hitting the buffet line—yet another ratcheting up of my worry. We grabbed plates and loaded them down, then caught each other up with what was going on with our lives while we munched our way through lunch. It was pleasant, but there was definitely an underlying tension in the air.

Finally, after finishing off the main course and grabbing yet another plate full of food from the dessert bar, I couldn't take the suspense any longer. "Okay, guys, just spill it already. What is it you two want?"

They looked at each other. What, did they really think I was so blind to their charms that I didn't know this was all leading to something? Arc might not have had a chance to get to know me that well yet, but Ruby sure as heck did.

Arc took a deep breath, then reached out to grab Ruby's hand on the table. Giving it a squeeze, he looked at me. Obviously, he was the chosen one to be their spokesperson. That actually surprised me. Ruby didn't give the reins over easily. She was a take-charge kind of gal if ever there was one.

"You know how things are kind of noisy and crowded at the farmhouse nowadays?" he asked. "Well, we have the perfect solution to that."

I felt my eyebrows raise. "You do?" My heart kind of sank a little. Maybe they didn't want anything after all. Maybe this was a mercy dinner to give me the bad news that Ruby was officially moving out. I wasn't all that sure I could handle that. I'd lived within a few steps of her room all of my life—even shared a space with her for most of it—and even now, with her room still holding all her things, it was her home.

Without her, would it still be home to me? I swallowed.

My expression must have given me away because Ruby reached out and grabbed my hand. Here we were sitting at a small table and all holding hands like we were trying to contact the other side or something. It was weird, and it didn't do a dang thing to ease my dread.

"I'm not leaving you, silly. I am leaving the farmhouse, yes." She looked over to give Arc a grin, then turned back to me. "But we want to bring you with us."

I just looked at them. They were a new couple basking in the honeymoon phase of a loving relationship. Why on earth would they want me along for the ride? Talk about uncomfortable living arrangements. Besides, Arc's apartment just wasn't all that big. I couldn't see how that would solve my overcrowding issues.

"We've found a house. Well, kind of sort of two houses, actually," Arc said, earning a glare from Ruby. He was too far gone to notice that though.

"You're buying a house together?" That was a big step. A really, really big step. Huge, even. It meant this would not be a short-lived thing. Not that I'd thought it would be. I had just been expecting them to take a little longer to get to this point.

Ruby's expression cleared, and she nodded. "We want to, yes, but we kind of need your help."

"My help? What the heck can I possibly do to help you buy a house?" Then I thought about it. "No way am I going to be the one to tell your mom. Not going to happen."

She laughed. "Not that kind of help, doofus. I'll do that part once the deal goes through. We want you to go in on buying the house with us."

I tilted my head at her. "You know I don't have that kind of money. My freelancing gigs cover my expenses, but that's about it. No way could I add a mortgage payment onto that, even if we were sharing it three ways." I mean, come on, Ruby knew that.

"That's okay because we have a plan. Don't we, Arc?" And the ball was back in his court just like that. They'd definitely rehearsed this more than once.

"We do. First of all, the owner is pretty desperate to sell. The house has been on the market for a couple of years now with no takers, and he's willing to do a deal. A small down payment, which Ruby and I can cover, and then basic rent payments for a year that go toward the purchase price. Again, we have the payments covered. It's actually less than my current place."

My eyebrows did their thing again. I still wasn't seeing where I fit into all this.

"It's what happens after that first year that we

need help with," Ruby said. "Once the year is up, we'll be facing a large balloon payment. If we can't make the payment, then the owner gets the house back, and we have to move out."

I tilted my head the other way. Still not getting it.

"I've been doing some research about your bounty hunting gigs, and I think we would make a great team. We could do a few jobs during the next year and come up with the payment easy."

Ah, the world made sense again.

"In fact, there is a large bounty open right now in Oak Hill that would pay out more than a third of what we would need. If we could bring him in, I'm pretty sure we could do this," Arc said, grinning.

"So, are you in?" Ruby asked.

Hunting bond jumpers was hard and dangerous work. Were they really up to it? I knew that Ruby had some martial arts in her background, like me, but what about Arc? Would he be a help or a liability?

I had to buy some time to think about this.

"I think before I agree to anything, I'd like to see this house. Or houses." I paused. "Are there really two of them?" That would make a difference on my end. A place of my very own had always kind of been a dream. Just one that I'd never thought might actually happen.

Arc hit the table in front of him. "We figured you'd want to see it. That's our next stop."

"You're going to love it," Ruby said, giving my hand another squeeze before letting it go.

Yeah, the jury was still out on that one. It would have to be a very special place indeed for me to be willing to turn my world upside down.

But then again, with the farmhouse and all its inhabitants at the moment, wasn't my world already topsy-turvy?

Chapter 2

We took my little doodlebug because of our two cars; it got the better gas mileage. Besides, it was kind of fun watching a tall man squeeze himself into the small backseat space of the bug. I know he's my brother and all, but Ruby had chosen well. My man wasn't the only one with a nice backside worth watching.

The house, or rather mini-estate as it turned out to be, was between the two towns of Wind's Crossing and Oak Hill. Right smack in the middle ground between the Ravenswind's farmhouse and the home—or rather mini-castle—that my parents now lived in. It got points on the plus side for that.

I added more points to the fact that it was in the country with no neighbors within sight of the place. The mini-estate came with five and a half acres, some of those partially wooded, a two-story cape cod home, and an old-fashioned barn out back.

Arc and Ruby were staying quiet about the barn. Kind of a 'you have to see it to believe it' kind of thing, according to them. I was trying to keep an open mind.

That wasn't hard once the place came into view. Once we got off the main highway, the road got a lot curvier. Obviously, the road makers out here didn't believe in straight lines. Some of the curves were ninety degree turns with trees on either side. Not a good road for speeding. Or driving after you've had a few at a local pub. The curvy road led to the entrance of the driveway, which was about the width of two cars, and right in the middle of a long line of tall and stately pine trees.

Privacy at its best.

It took another few seconds after turning carefully onto the drive before I got my first glimpse of the house. All I could say was wow. And that was more of an in my own head kind of thing. The place kind of left me speechless.

I parked next to a black Lincoln in the driveway, and we all climbed out. I was so impressed with the surroundings that I didn't even watch Arc maneuver himself out of my car. That's saying something right there.

The house looked freshly painted, and the windows all had decorative shutters of a bright and cheerful blue. The covered front porch stretched from one end of the house to the next and even rounded the corner and led to a door more to the rear of the house.

I thought I saw movement in one of the upstairs dormer windows, but then we didn't expect the place to be empty, did we? The owner was there to show us around. Personally, I could have done without that part. Especially after meeting the man.

We didn't even make it to the front steps before he came around the side of the house, almost at a dead run. He stopped short when he saw us, and straightened, giving a quick glance behind him before straightening his tie and giving us a shaky smile.

"Was something chasing you?" Arc asked.

It was a good question. I mean, the man was definitely acting a little scared. But all I saw behind him was a woman about my age. And she didn't look a bit scary to me. She was dressed in jeans and a flannel shirt, much like my current outfit, and she wasn't holding a knife or a gun or anything.

What was his problem?

The man gave a shaky laugh. "No, not at all, I just, uh, I thought I heard you pull in and I didn't want to miss you." He took a deep breath and held out his hand to me. "I'm Kyle Jordan, the owner of this place. You must be Amie."

Well, if I must... I hesitated but finally took his hand for a quick shake. Something about this guy was giving me the serious creeps. Call it intuition or something. I'd learned to trust that feeling over the years. It was usually spot on. If this man was the one offering the contract, I'd definitely want Merlin or Archimedes Senior to take a look at it before any of us signed on that dotted line.

"Come this way, and I'll unlock the front door for you." He straightened his tie again. "Um, I'm running late for a meeting in Oak Hill. It, um, came up at the last minute. Would you all mind terribly if I ran off on you? You could just maybe lock up for me before you leave?"

That sounded a bit weird to me, but I wasn't going to look a gift horse in the mouth. Neither, apparently were Arc and Ruby. We waved him off down the driveway and then stepped into the house.

Nothing out of the ordinary. It was clean, and the carpet didn't look like it had seen much use, so it had to be fairly new. Long, sturdy drapes hung from all the windows, tied back to show an inset of filmy lightweight sheers. Enough to keep anyone outside from seeing in, but not enough to keep out the sunlight.

It was... homey. The downstairs was the main living area with a large entryway and living room, a full kitchen complete with one of those fancy island type cooking surfaces, a dining room, and a den. Pretty much the equivalent to the whole downstairs of the farmhouse, but all one big living space, not divided into two separate ones.

So this was how normal families lived. Huh.

There was also a half bath hidden under a rather ornate staircase. Tiny, but there was enough room for a toilet and a small pedestal sink. That's really all you needed most of the time, wasn't it? It was just enough to keep any guests one might have over from having to invade the more personal space upstairs. The bedrooms.

There were three total rooms up there. Six if you counted bathrooms. Did bathrooms count when you were counting rooms in a house? I didn't think they did, so yeah, three rooms upstairs.

They'd all been meant to be bedrooms, I'm sure, but one of them had been redesigned as an office. Or maybe a more accurate description would be a library with a desk. I kind of loved it. The rest of the house was empty. Not this room. There was a large oak desk on one side of the room and a high-top oak table with two matching chairs on the other side. And surrounding it all? On every available inch of wall space not taken by a window or door, there were bookshelves. Floor to ceiling bookshelves. It was truly a sight to behold.

Miraculously, the shelves were still loaded down with the previous owner's books. It looked as though this room had been recently used too. More like someone had just stepped out of it to retrieve coffee and a light snack. It definitely didn't feel right being here in an empty house devoid of both people and furnishings.

"You love it, don't you?" Ruby was bouncing on her heels. "You don't even need to say it. I can see it in your face. You love it. I knew you would. That's why I saved this room for last."

Well, yeah, of course, I loved it. This room had my name written all over it. The only thing missing was my rainbow-colored bean bag chair. There was even a perfect spot for it right there in the far corner.

And how could I deny that my hands were literally itching to get their fingers on all those lovely books? I could spend hours just going through them.

But this house wouldn't be mine, would it? This would be Ruby's and Arc's. I was pretty sure the barn would be my place. If we did this thing. That was still up for debate. Besides, surely the owner would come and take all this away before we moved in. Then it would just be a normal, everyday room with four walls. Much less magical to me.

"Everything in here stays right where it is too," Arc said.

Am I that easy to read? I just looked at him. "No way would the owner want to part with all this."

He shrugged. "He says this stuff reminds him too much of his sister. I'm guessing the two of them really didn't get along all that well. One of the reasons he says he wants to sell it rather than live here himself."

I raised my eyebrow at him. "And did he say what was stopping him from selling it?" I ran my hand over the desk. It was a high-quality desk. Much nicer than anything I was used to. Or could afford. It would bring a pretty penny at Opal's shop.

Arc hesitated, for the first time looking a little unsure. "Actually, no, he didn't."

"Now, Amie, what have our moms taught us about gift horses? Just take this as a win. What could be better than a house with an already furnished library, right? You can always switch out the books as you go to make it more yours."

I swallowed and looked away. As much as I loved this room, I couldn't see myself invading the new couple's privacy on a daily basis just to hang out here. But maybe, if they were willing, we could somehow move all this out to the barn?

Taking a deep breath, I turned to Ruby. "I think it's time to see the barn."

She glanced over at Arc and then back to me. "But you love the house, right? I mean you could totally see yourself living here, couldn't you?"

My eyebrows were really getting a workout today. Why had they mentioned two houses (or sort of houses), if they'd planned on all of us living together under the same roof? I thought that had implied a place of my own. Had I gotten that wrong?

"Yes, I love the house." I hesitated. "But I'm sure the barn will be just as nice." Another not so covert glance between the two of them. "Okay, guys, what are you not telling me?"

Arc sighed. "Well, we were kind of hoping you'd want the house. I mean, it would be perfect for you and Opie."

If my eyebrows rose any higher, they'd go flying off my face. When did Opie moving in with me come into play? I really didn't think he was quite up to taking that step yet. And why were they bringing that up now?

Ruby laughed. "You don't know her too well, do you?" She gave Arc a light pat on the shoulder. "Now you've got her mind going off in a totally different direction. We need her focused on this for a little while longer, dum-dum."

Color rose on his cheeks, and he looked away. "Sorry. My bad. Shouldn't have brought Opie into this, should I?"

"Probably not," I said slowly. But, of course, now that the words had been said, I could see their worth. This place would be an awesome home to start a family in. Not that I was any readier for that step than Opie was. I wasn't.

But Ruby and Arc were. They were already planning to move in together. And the Goddess had more than hinted that there would be children involved at some point in their future. Although she had failed to mention just how far into the future that would happen.

"I can see the wheels spinning, so I will be totally straight with you." Ruby smiled at me. "Arc and I really, really want the barn. I was kind of hoping if we got you to fall in love with the house, you wouldn't mind us taking it so bad."

Was she saying the barn was nicer than all of this? No bloody way.

"I really think it's time to see this barn." This time my words got a little more action.

We made our way down the stairs and out past the front porch, which I was totally picturing all decked out. That was another thing we'd have to consider. Furniture. Furnishing an entire house wouldn't be cheap. I could see a lot of work in the next year just to raise the money for the balloon payment. Add in buying furniture and porch stuff, and I'd be working around the clock.

Was I ready for that? Would the two of them actually help out? Or would they end up being more of a hindrance? Unfortunately, the only way to find that out was to try it.

The barn was quite a distance from the house. Houses in town were much closer together than these two buildings were. Privacy in spades here. Even from each other.

The outside of the barn wasn't anything really special. It was large and old-fashioned, with glistening wood. The place had obviously been well taken care of, but at the end of the day, it was still just a barn.

That is, until you looked inside it.

Glistening wood everywhere. A rustic feel with open beams and cedar paneling. A twisting solid oak banister lining the staircase to an upper level. It was totally unbelievable.

Ruby had done well to show me the house first. She was a pretty dang smart cookie, my cousin.

"Okay," I said, steeling myself. "Let's talk numbers. If I think this is something we can really pull off, I'm in." I mean, how sad would it be to move in and fall in love with the place only to lose it months later? That wasn't something I was willing to risk.

I could really grow to love it here.

It was perfect. And yes, deep down inside me, somewhere around the general area of my heart, I was really hoping that Opie would feel the same way.

Chapter 3

The numbers seemed doable, if a little scary. There were a lot more digits involved than I was used to working with. Bottom line, after the small down payment and the year's worth of 'rent' payments, we'd still need to come up with about a hundred grand for that hefty balloon payment.

With three of us working together on this, it could be doable, but that didn't mean that it wasn't terrifying at the same time. If we ended up not being able to come up with the money in time, we'd be left with two choices. Either we'd lose the house, or we'd have to go begging to our parents for a loan.

No way was any of us financially solvent enough to qualify for a bank loan. Then again, maybe in a year, we would be. If it came to that. I was really hoping that it wouldn't.

The other, and perhaps even more so, terrifying thought about all of this was telling Opal. I was pretty sure that Mom would be cool with it. After all, she'd been the first to leave the farmhouse to form her own, new family. Surely Opal realized that eventually Ruby and I would have to do the same.

Maybe, now that I think about it, that's why she'd moved in Kimberly and her children. Not to mention the fact that she was well into the process of formally adopting Nancy. Maybe she was moving ahead too, and I just hadn't realized it until now.

Even so, the thought of telling her wasn't a pleasant one. And no way was I doing it without Ruby.

"So, how do we do this?" Ruby asked looking over at me.

We'd just hit Wind's Crossing and were almost back to the farmhouse. And Opal.

I glanced at her and then back at the road. "She's your mom. I think you need to call the shots on this one."

"You would." She looked out the passenger side window, and a minute passed by in silence. "Do you think she will be upset?"

I thought about it and then shook my head. "No, I really don't. I mean, it's not like you've been spending all that much time at the farmhouse lately anyway, right? She has to know this was coming." I paused. "Although adding me into the mix will probably come as a bit of a shock."

Then again, it was Opal we were talking about. So maybe not.

I pulled around back and parked by the Meditation Garden. That was something I would miss. Dearly. Too bad we couldn't take it with us.

Of course, we could always build another one at the new place, once we became the full and legal owners. But it just wouldn't be the same. This one had been built out of friendship and love with Billy Myers' own two hands, and even a little help from us.

My cousin and I are a lot alike. Where my mind went, hers was pretty sure to follow.

"How is Billy doing?"

I lifted a shoulder and blinked back a tear. "As well as can be expected, I guess. Archie... Dad... at least got the judge to agree to a minimum-security prison for him. And he has access to books and stuff. They are letting him get some therapy too. The next decade will be rough on him, but it's Billy. He'll be fine."

I hoped. Billy was special in a lot of ways. And right now, I was feeling guilty about not having paid him a visit in over a month. It wasn't all that short of a drive. But something I'd need to make sure happened soon.

Nancy and Mason came running down the steps. What they had been doing up there, I didn't know. They didn't really have any reason to be up there as that was where our apartments were. And obviously, we weren't home.

"Don't be mad, okay?" Nancy said.

That didn't sound good.

"What are we not to be mad about?"

She gave Mason a look and then took a deep breath. "We got some train tracks and trains and stuff from a garage sale. Auntie wouldn't let us set them up in the house because she didn't want to have to step over them."

My heart started beating a little faster. "You set them up in my apartment?" That was so not cool.

Nancy stood a little straighter. "Of course not! We wouldn't go in there with you gone." Then the color rose in her cheeks. "Besides, your apartment is in the house, isn't it?"

Ruby groaned. "There are train tracks all over our balcony, aren't there?"

Oh, crap. That was almost as bad. Good thing

we had the inside stairs to use. And maybe a really good thing that we were making this move. Funny how the farmhouse had always seemed so huge until we had added children into the mix of people living there. Now, it was shrinking on what seemed to be a daily basis.

Ruby and I looked at each other. We had every right to be mad, but what good would it do? Kids had to play somewhere. And a train set sounded like fun, even to me. Ruby and I would just have to watch our step for a while.

"It's okay," I finally told them. "But when you're finished playing, make sure you move everything over to the side farthest from the steps, okay? I don't want to trip on a train after dark and take a tumble down the stairs." And I didn't want anyone else doing that either.

Opie came to mind. He was my most regular after-dark visitor, after all. I really didn't want him to have to go on medical leave again because of me and my family.

"You mean we can keep it set up?" Mason sounded excited. "That'd be great!" Then he was tugging on Nancy's arm to get her back up the stairs.

She grinned over at us and mouthed, "Thank you." Then the two of them were headed back up at a dead run.

"Use the rails!" I shouted after them. I didn't want either of them to take a tumble either.

We turned the corner of the house toward the front door and almost ran smack dab into Opal. From the somewhat guilty look on her face, I could tell she'd been listening. And that she'd expected us to follow the kids rather than head for the front door. Well, surprise, Opal, we're coming to have a little chat.

"Thanks for that," she said. "I wasn't all that sure how you two would react to your balcony becoming the kids' Grand Central Station."

She led the way back inside and seemed startled when we went to follow her into her apartment. "Were you two coming to see me?"

Ruby gave a big swallow and then nodded. "Yes. We have something we need to talk to you about."

Opal looked at Ruby and then over at me. "Why do I have a feeling it's about something I'm not going to like all that well? Have you girls gone and gotten yourself in trouble again?" She rubbed her hand down her face. "Please don't tell me that there's another dead body involved."

"No dead bodies," I said. Not yet, anyway. I was kind of hoping we got to keep saying that for a really long time. We'd been through a lot in the past year. And I'd seen more than my fair share of bodies to last me a lifetime. Of course, now that I was a contract employee of the Wind's Crossing Sheriff's Department, I was sure I'd be seeing more. Hopefully, just on the other side of my camera though. Not up close and personal.

"Well, that's a relief," she said. She headed over to her favorite chair and sat down. After a second or two of mental debate, Ruby and I sat on the couch.

The house was quiet. Too quiet.

"Where are Kimberly and the baby?" I asked.

"They had a play date." She shook her head. "Why a six-week-old needs a play date, I'm sure I don't know. But, according to one of the new books Kimberly's been reading, it's important to add social activity at a very young age." Her steely eyes locked on Ruby. "So, spill it already before you have a stroke."

"Arc and I found a house. Actually, two houses in one, with land and everything. And we want to go in with Amy and buy it." She said it all in a rush, then sat there and stared at her mom. Goddess help me, but she looked so tense that if Opal sneezed, I think she'd have bolted for the door.

Opal must have thought so too and decided to take pity on her. "Well, I can't say the moving out thing surprises me, as I've been expecting that news for a while now. But the buying a house thing is kind of a new twist." She tilted her head at Ruby. "Are you two sure you're ready for that big of a step?"

Ruby nodded. "We are, Mom. And it will actually be the three of us."

Opal's eyes traveled over to me, and I caught a little of Ruby's tension. Please, Goddess, don't let her blame me for all of this. After all, it was my brother that was taking her daughter away from her. And I'm the one that had brought him into our lives. It had been an accident on my part—a carefully planned Goddess accident, but still. In a small way, this was all on me. Okay, maybe not such a small way. This was all on me.

Luckily, the look she was giving me wasn't a bad one. In fact, it looked almost... friendly.

"Well, as long as the two of you are sticking together, then you should be fine." She took a deep breath. "I feel kind of bad changing things up around here without consulting you girls first. I shouldn't have done that."

"That's not what this is about!" Ruby and I spoke at the same time.

Opal shook her head. "I never said it was, children. I was just stating a fact." She chewed her lip for a minute. "Actually, this could end up being a really good thing for all of us. I kind of miss having the downstairs as my own private domain, and if I moved Kimberly and the children upstairs... well, the nights would be quieter down here too."

A funny feeling started creeping into the pit of my stomach. We weren't even out of the house yet, and she was already giving our rooms away? What if this didn't work out? What if in a year from now we didn't have the money in hand, and we needed to move back in?

It was starting to sound like failure would not be an option.

Chapter 4

If Ruby was as shocked by Opal's statement as I was, she sure as bloody heck wasn't showing it. But then, she had Arc to help out with a place to stay if it didn't work. Then I realized something important. Even if we couldn't come up with the full hundred grand, we'd at least have a good pile of money by the end of a year's time. Enough to pay rent at a new place for sure. Or buy a little smaller place.

But where would thoughts like that lead me? I was better back at the failure wasn't an option kind of thinking. We'd make this work. One way or another.

Opal stood to go and start dinner, and Ruby went with her. For once they gave me a pass in the dinner preparation. Good thing too. I had another pressing engagement upstairs to get to.

I had to tell Destiny. And get her opinion on the whole moving out thing.

As technically she was a bit higher up on the

food chain than Opal was, I probably should have started with her. But then again, it was the Goddess who made me who I was. And I was a witch that put family above all else. Even, Goddess help me, Her. I was resting in the knowledge that if she hadn't wanted me to be that way, I wouldn't be.

I climbed the stairs slowly, thinking about how the next hour or so was going to go. If I had to rely on simple yes and no answers to my questions, this would be a lengthy process. And I was bound to miss something important.

The mental debate had been going on for a while now inside my head. It was time. I was terrified and nervous as all bloody get out, but it was time to let Destiny into my mind.

Truthfully, she was probably already there, but I hadn't allowed the two-way conversational abilities yet. By the time I reached the top of the stairs, my heart was racing and my breathing was off the charts. The first thing I had to do was grab a paper bag and get my breathing under control before I fainted. It had been a while since that kind of thing had happened.

When your life seems to be in a pretty constant state of tension, for some reason there are fewer panic attacks. Weird but true. At least it seemed to be for me.

By the time my breathing was back to normal, Destiny was sitting at my feet staring up at me. When my breathing started speeding up again, she jumped into my lap and rested her front paws on my chest. A lot of my tension fell away. Not all of it, but enough for me to do this thing.

I took a deep breath and looked her dead in the eyes. "If I agree to do the whole mind message thing, and it doesn't work out, can I reverse it?"

She looked as sad as a cat could look and wagged her tail. No. Once done, going back wasn't an option. We'd be opening a door that couldn't be closed.

Another minute of staring into those beautiful tiny green eyes, and it didn't really matter anymore. "Okay, can I at least ask you to only use it when absolutely necessary? Or when I come to you for a conversation?"

The meow I got for that one was so much more than a simple yes. Talk about being put into your place by a cat. Well, a very special cat, but a cat all the same.

My question had been more than a bit presumptuous. I mean, it was the Goddess we were talking about. Surely, she had far better things to do than sit and chat with me all day. I got that. My worry was how much of my cat was Goddess and how much was pure cat. It was the cat part that worried me.

But I had gotten the meow and that, to me, was a promise. I just hoped familiars took promises as much to heart as witches did. Time would tell, I guess.

"Okay, then how do we go about this?"

Destiny tilted her head at me and then gave a cat sigh. Jumping down, she crossed the room to my beanbag chair. That was my favorite place to meditate. Comfort at its finest in my opinion.

Within seconds, I was in my sanctuary with the Goddess standing before me. Her sheer beauty never failed to take my breath away. Destiny was there too, sitting calmly at my feet.

"Are you sure you are ready for this?" The Goddess looked deep into my eyes. "Once your mind is opened to me, there is no going back."

I swallowed but nodded. "I'm ready. I think. I mean, it's not like I can just drop everything I'm doing and come here to talk, is it? Or expect you to be here all the time for me. But I have a question if you don't mind."

She smiled. "Ask."

"You said a small part of you is in Destiny. If I talk with her, will it be the same as talking to you?"

Her eyebrow arched. "Yes and no." She thought for a minute. Probably trying to figure out how to instill a part of the wisdom of Gods down to where a mere mortal would be capable of understanding. "It's kind of like your computers these days. If it helps, you can think of Destiny as a kind of very special programmed copy of me. Not exactly me, but a program that I can access and update at any time." She paused and then nodded. "Yes, that's about as close as I can get to how it works."

"Okay," I said, drawing that word out as long as I could to give me time to think. "But she is still a cat too, right?"

Destiny rubbed against my legs and started purring.

"Well, as I don't generally purr unless there is a handsome God involved, I'd think that answers your question."

"So she's… what… fifty percent cat? Seventy-five?" I was really trying hard to grasp this. Or, just maybe, I was trying really hard to postpone the inevitable.

"She's all cat. Every last little strand of fur is one hundred percent cat. But she is a very special cat. One that can help you when you need it." She stared hard into my eyes. "She is not me. It is important that you understand that. To do that would be against the rules and open far too many doors to the side we oppose."

I nodded. "She's just a cat. A special cat, but just a cat." I paused. "Really?"

The Goddess laughed. "I would never lie to you, child. I might not be in a position to tell you everything you may wish to know, but I would never lie."

I took a deep breath and squared my shoulders.

"Thank you. Okay, so now I'm ready."

She led me through it. The whole process was a very simple one, much like my analogy of opening a door. A brain door, if you will.

I'd expected everything to change with the opening of my mind, but everything felt exactly the same. I was exactly the same.

Looking down at Destiny, I asked. "Did it work?"

Meow.

Crapsnackles. I'd done all this for nothing?

"It worked, silly. I was just messing with you."

Great. I don't just have a very special cat programmed with a copy of the Goddess herself.

I have a very special cat programmed with a copy of the Goddess herself that thinks it has a sense of humor. And attitude.

Goddess help me.

Chapter 5

It shouldn't have really surprised me that Destiny was one hundred percent behind the move. After all, someone higher up had made Arc and Ruby aware of this estate being for sale. And the well below market value selling price fairly reeked of the Goddess' influence.

Well, truthfully, it fairly reeked anyway. In a much too good to be true kind of way. I mean, who sells a house with a fully remodeled and totally awesome barn at that price? With land to boot? I'd be wanting a full home inspection before we signed any legal paperwork.

There was definitely something that the current owner wasn't telling us. Better to find out what that was before we became the new owners. Owners-to-be, anyway. I wasn't all that up on how contracts worked. Were we the owners as soon as we signed? Or did we only become owners once we paid the contract out in full?

Lucky for us Arc's family were high-priced lawyers, huh?

After my little conference with the Goddess, Destiny and I went down to join the others for supper. After that, Arc and Opie came over, and we crashed in my tiny little apartment to hang out and watch a movie. I'd always been comfortable in my little space. But now that I had seen the possible future and what it might hold in the way of room, the walls seemed to be shrinking in on me.

So, the next morning, we hit the ground running. First up was a quick visit to Mineheart Law to have Merlin go over the contract. According to him, it was nearly perfect. By the time he was finished with it, it was even better. Nothing really changed. There were just a couple fewer loopholes for the current owner to use to regain the house.

Then Merlin even went one step further and called in a favor with a prior client of his. He managed to get the man to agree to do a full home inspection by the end of the day. Not a small feat, that, since it was Sunday.

As it stood now, the only thing that would stop us from owning that estate, pending a good word from the inspector, was if we couldn't come up with that large balloon payment at the end of a year.

Our next stop would hopefully take care of that.

I'd grown used to dealing with Boswell Bonds. No, it wasn't exactly a good working relationship, but I knew what to expect from him. Which was basically nothing. I was comfortable with that. No surprises there.

But in our small hometown, there just weren't enough bond jumpers to come even close to giving us the funds we needed. There were barely enough to pay my meager living expenses as they currently were. We'd have to go further afield to make this work.

TideWell Bonds was the biggest agency in Oak Hill. We started there.

Arc had read in the papers about a felon who had recently skipped on a very large bail bond. If we could manage to get the standard ten percent, we'd have a tidy amount to cover our move-in expenses, buy some furniture, and even start the savings account for that future balloon with a bang.

Of course, I didn't think we'd be getting anything even close to that. I know my first job with Boswell hadn't paid nearly that well. I didn't see this one going any better than that had.

But then, we did have some things going for us that I hadn't had back then. My experience and Ruby's negotiation skills. She was a true master of the art.

We dressed up in black jeans and leather jackets just to make us appear a bit tougher. Ruby and I aren't all that impressive height and muscle wise, and we needed all the help we could get. Arc, outfitted in his black get-up was impressive as heck. He was the apparent muscle of the group.

I'd had Boswell call ahead and give a reference for me. When I saw the grin on Mr. Vincent's face when we walked in, I started to doubt whether that had been a good move. Who knows what Boswell had told the guy? From the look on his face, their conversation hadn't been solely about my stellar work history and unbroken record of getting my man.

Kind of like the Canadian Mounties, I was. I always got my man. Or woman. I really wasn't choosy about the contracts I took as long as they paid out in the end. After all, they were the ones who had broken the law. I was just the one who would make sure they paid the price for it.

I was cool with that.

"I've been expecting you," Mr. Vincent said.

His voice had a hint of laughter in it. He was enjoying this. "Please, come into my office."

His place was a far cry from Boswell's little basement office. Here, we were on street level, and he had a receptionist, a private office, and everything. It impressed me. Maybe we could get that ten percent after all. It was obvious the man was doing well for himself.

Once we were seated, the man smiled at us from behind his desk. "So, Amie, I take it you've branched out and into team work?"

"Yes, sir." I nodded at Arc and Ruby. "They each bring something special to the table. I think you'll find my team to be super effective in bringing in the bond jumpers."

He chuckled. "Oh, I've heard of your reputation for being an ace bounty hunter. It's amusing that now there are three of you."

I didn't like how this was going. Apparently, neither did Ruby because that's when she stepped in. Good thing too. I was kind of volatile in situations like this. I take my reputation seriously.

"Mr. Vincent, before we waste time here, are you willing to give us a shot at working with you or not? If not, we thank you for your time, but there are other places we could be visiting right now."

His chuckle grew. "Believe me, I wouldn't want to miss out on the opportunity to work with such an… interesting crew as yourselves. In fact, I have the perfect case for you all to cut your teeth on."

"We already have a case in mind," Ruby said. Her voice was firm. "We want to bring in Michael Gray."

Vincent's eyes widened, and he leaned back in his chair with a low whistle. "You three really are the aggressive little bounty hunters, aren't you? You do know that Gray is a very bad man, right? I still don't know how his attorney ever got the court to agree to let the man go on bail. Let alone one so small."

I had to work to keep my facial expression set. Vincent considered a quarter million dollar bond small? Were we that far out of our league here?

Ruby never batted an eye. She was cool as a cucumber, and all the other clichés that go along those same lines. She stared him right in the eyes.

"We can handle it, believe me." She paused briefly. "But we want the standard fee of ten percent and not a penny less."

Now his chuckle turned into a belly laugh. "Oh, that's rich. The three of you have yet to bring in a single capture, and you want full rates? I have guys who've worked for me for years and still don't get that high of a percentage." His eyes traveled over each of us in turn.

Ruby, the negotiator, Arc, the muscle, and me, the old-pro. That's what I considered myself at this point, anyway. With five captures under my belt, I thought I deserved the title of experience. Besides, it was pretty much all I had going for me.

Finally, he leaned forward. "I'll offer you two percent."

It was Ruby's time to laugh, and she did. Then she stood. "I thought maybe you were serious about wanting to work with us, but I guess not. We're leaving."

Vincent waved her back down or tried to. She wasn't budging, but she wasn't walking toward the door either.

"I can go three, but that's as high as I've ever offered an untested bounty hunter."

"But you aren't getting just one bounty hunter," Ruby said calmly. "You're getting a team. Amie's methods might not be all that orthodox, but you have to admit she has a good history of getting the job done, no matter what it takes. I assure you, the addition of the two of us to her team only strengthens it. And we wouldn't dream of taking less than five percent. Not for the danger this one entails. Anything less is ludicrous."

He leaned back again, a calculating look in his eyes. I could see the wheels turning in his mind. "Sorry, I can't do it. But I thank you all for coming in."

Ah well, it had been worth a shot. I stood and followed Ruby to the door. I could see from Arc's face that he wasn't happy that we were leaving, but he'd been told upfront that Ruby was in charge of the negotiation part of things.

Sure enough, we barely made it to his office door before Vincent broke. "Look, I can go as high as three and a half percent, but that really is my highest offer."

Here's the thing. We'd all agreed going in that if we could get Vincent up to over three percent, we'd take it. It was better than what I'd been paid for my first job, and this one was a lot bigger. Besides, this was all about building a reputation as a team. If we succeeded with this high-profile job, we'd be on the map.

So Arc was probably surprised that when he opened his mouth to agree to Vincent's terms, I stepped on his foot. Hard.

He yelped, and I put my hand on his arm. "Oh, I'm so sorry. We'd better go out and make sure I didn't break anything." Then I gave Ruby a nod and dragged him outside, through the receptionist area and out the front door.

"What the hell was that about?" Arc asked, rubbing the top of his foot as best he could through the sneakers. If he'd been wearing hiking books like me and Ruby, my stomp wouldn't have been nearly as effective. Personally, I was kind of glad about his footwear choice for the day. Might not have gotten his attention in time otherwise.

"You were about to take his deal."

"Well, yeah, but we'd all agreed…" His voice trailed off and his eyes widened. "You really think Ruby can do better than that?"

I shrugged. "Doesn't really matter what I think. Only what Ruby thinks. And she hadn't said yes yet." I nodded down at his foot. "Believe me, you should be thanking me right now. You and Ruby haven't had a big fight yet, have you?"

Not that I really had to ask. If they had, I would have heard all about it from Ruby. We might not be seeing as much of each other right now, but there were still cell phones.

The color drained from his face. "She'd have been totally pissed at me, wouldn't she?"

"You have no idea. She takes these things very seriously."

He gulped and nodded. "Thanks." Then he wiggled his foot. "At least I don't think anything is broken, but it's definitely going to bruise."

"I've got something for that." I led him over to a bench out in front of the office and instructed him to take off his shoe while I dug through my pack. I'd learned a long time ago to always keep some of Mom's Miracle Healing Salve with me. It earned its name.

Mom was an awesome healer.

I pulled down his sock and rubbed a generous amount of the salve over the reddened area. His quick intake of breath told me that the effect was almost instant. It usually was.

"That's your mom's recipe, isn't it?"

Well, yeah. But now that I thought about it, I needed to have her teach it to me, along with the spell that went with it. The Goddess had said I was in training right now. We all were. But she'd also said it wouldn't be a bad idea to learn the art of healing from Mom. I just hadn't pulled that particular trigger yet. Too many things happening far too close together to give me the time.

That needed to change. It wouldn't do to ignore a direct recommendation from the Goddess for too long. That kind of thing would bite you in the heiny in the end.

It wasn't long before Ruby came out the doors behind us with a big grin on her face.

"You did it, didn't you?" Arc asked. "You got the old goat to give us more?"

Pride was all over her face as she nodded. "A full seven percent." Then her grin dimmed a little. "But don't get super excited. It's not the Michael Gray case. He wouldn't go over four on that one. Not on our first run. But we made a deal. If the Gemstone Team can bring in this one, he'll give us the go-ahead to work on the Gray case for a five percent cut."

"Why not the full seven he's giving us on this one?" I asked. If the percentage would be based on the bond amount, that smelt like bad business to me. I mean, if this one was a lot smaller bond, then we'd stand to make more money at four percent on the other one. Surely, Ruby saw that, right?

For once, she hesitated. I was starting to think she'd been blinded by the percentage number rather than the final fee. "Well…"

Okay, it wouldn't do to have our chief negotiator start questioning her skills. Besides, all we had to do was bring in this one little jumper—hopefully, a much easier one than Gray would be—and we'd be off and running with another few grand added to the fee for Gray.

It didn't sound so terrible when I thought of it like that. Maybe I was questioning Ruby's skill far too soon.

"I think you did a great job," I said, throwing my

arm around her shoulders. "And now that we've got him to agree to five percent on a big job, he shouldn't be able to drop our fee after that. Only raise it, right? I still don't make that much from Boswell." Or at least I hadn't. I had a feeling that would change next time he called me with a case.

Arc pulled up his sock and put his shoe back on. "So, who are we going after? Is it a dangerous one?"

She shook her head. "Shouldn't be dangerous. This one doesn't have a history of violence. Just burglary and theft."

Arc stopped in mid-motion. "Oh, Goddess no. Please tell me he didn't just hire us to bring in Jack Watson."

Ruby frowned. I was getting a really bad feeling about this. And just when things were going so well too.

"That's the name all right. But why is that a bad thing?"

"It's bad because we've just agreed to hunt down my Uncle Jack. Oh, Merlin will not be happy about this. At all."

Wait a minute. We had an Uncle Jack?

Chapter 6

I was thinking maybe Uncle Jack was from his mother's side of the family, but come to find out, Jack Watson wasn't blood relation at all. He was a college buddy of Merlin that was, according to Arc, closer to them than most families could brag. Sometimes friendship can be just as thick as blood. At least when it came to the Minehearts.

"We have to talk with Merlin," Arc said. "This is really bad, guys."

Ruby looked at me and then back at him. "But we're still bringing him in, right? I mean it might upset your uncle—or rather uncles—but the fact remains that if he did the crime, he needs to do the time. I mean, your folks are lawyers. Surely, they'll understand that, right?"

Arc didn't look nearly so sure.

"I'm thinking we need to know what the heck happened before we go rushing into anything," I said. "Why don't we go to the library and look at the papers and see what the deal is?"

Ruby gave me a weird look. "Why would we do

that?"

I mirrored her look right back to her. "To find out why he was arrested and to see if maybe there was something hanky about it. Some reason for him to be running."

"No, I know why we need to look at the papers, but why would we go to the library?" She lifted the file in her hands. "It's all in here."

All I could do was stare at the file. "It is?" She handed it to me, and I popped it open and started flipping through the paperwork inside. It was a true thing of beauty. Not only was there a copy of all the police reports on his latest crime, but there were also printouts of all the news coverage covering it too.

Crapsnackles. Was this the normal for Vincent? If so, I was definitely impressed. Having this kind of information right out of the gate was a luxury I'd never had before.

"Okay, change of plans," I said slowly, my eyes still traveling over the articles. "We go to a coffee shop and look over all this stuff, then come up with a plan."

"We really need to talk with Merlin." Arc was sounding a bit like a broken record. If anyone still had vinyl that did that anymore. Maybe I needed to update my metaphors. Or maybe I just needed to say flat out that he kept repeating himself. A lot.

"We'll talk to him all right." My voice wasn't wishy-washy either. I meant every word of it. I had fallen in love with that stupid house, and I wanted to make this work. Most of all, right now looking at this gloriously full file folder in my hands, I wanted to continue to work for Vincent. This was so much better than anything I'd ever gotten from Boswell.

"Come on, Arc," Ruby said, reaching down a hand to him on the bench. "You know Amie's right. We need to see exactly what we're dealing with before we go and upset your uncle."

He hesitated, then nodded. "Okay. As long as the two of you agree that he is definitely on the agenda for this evening."

Oak Hill didn't have a Flour Pot, unfortunately, but they did have one of those ultra-modern big chain coffee shops. Not my personal favorite, but it would have to do. The important thing was that they had a small table in the corner open. It wasn't their busiest time of the day, so as long as we kept our voices down, we should be okay. Especially since most of the people in the shop seemed to be working on their laptops with headphones firmly in place.

Privacy in the midst of a crowd. Years ago, that wouldn't even have been possible. I would have found the lack of social interaction sad on most days. But today it worked for me.

According to the file, Jack Watson was a stellar thief. He'd been arrested five times before and done time for two of them. On every single case, Merlin Mineheart was listed as the attorney of record. There was a note in the file that with this crime, Jack could be found to be a career criminal and the sentence he got might be a very long one.

Hence, the running part.

"There's something not right here," Arc said, frowning. "Jack's always owned up and done the time. He went to all his court appearances and took what he deserved. This isn't right."

I tapped the part about the career criminal. "But he had Uncle Merlin as a lawyer, and he knew the sentence wouldn't be all that long. They always made a plea deal." Some of the deals even seemed a little too good to be true, honestly. Merlin had to be one heck of a good lawyer. I'd keep that in mind should I ever need one.

"Read back that article on this latest burglary. Skip to the part where they found the evidence linking it to Jack."

I searched through the paperwork until I found it and then started reading. "An arrest was made today on the case of the missing diamond necklace taken from the mayor's wife. Police say that the necklace, worth over twenty-five thousand dollars, was recovered at the home of a known thief, Jack Watson. Watson has denied any knowledge of the crime and stated that he has no idea how the jewelry came to be in his home. However, it should be noted that Mr. Watson has done prison time for this type of crime before. The police seem certain they have the right burglar. Of course, it will take a trial for a decisive answer to the case."

It took a lot to impress me when it came to newspaper articles, but this one, short as it was, did. The reporter seemed to keep to the facts, rather than put any kind of personal slant to it. That was rare these days.

Looking back up at Arc, I had to ask. "So what doesn't seem right about it?"

He shook his head. "Can't put my finger on it, but it sounds… off. Can we please go talk to Merlin now?"

To give him credit, he had been pretty patient with us going over the file. I glanced at Ruby and she nodded.

Time to visit Uncle Merlin.

***

It might sound funny, but this was the first time I'd ever been to Merlin's place. I'd always seen him either at Mom and Archie's or at Lily's. Whatever I had pictured as his home in my mind's eye, this wasn't it.

His brother, and now my mom, lived in nothing

less than a mansion. Merlin's abode was a lot humbler. It was still beautiful, don't get me wrong, but much more down to earth. The house was just outside of city limits, and it was made of wood. As in logs.

My fancy-pants Uncle Merlin lived in a log cabin. Why had anyone not ever told me that? It was actually kind of cool. In all my life, I'd only ever seen them from the outside. I was looking forward to totally checking this one out thoroughly. Maybe I could even get Merlin to give me a tour.

If he wasn't too ticked off about the whole us trying to bring his best friend to justice thing.

At our knock, the door swung open almost instantly. Merlin had to have some kind of early warning spell in place to alert him to visitors. He smiled at us and stepped back to let us in.

"To what do I owe this pleasant surprise visit?" Then he must have seen the look on Arc's face and his smile dimmed. "Oh no, so this isn't just a pleasant social call, is it? Well, come on in then and let's get to it."

Arc stepped through the doorway first. In his obvious confusion, he'd forgotten the old rule of ladies first. It was just as well.

Ruby and I were stopped in our tracks. As in, we couldn't pass the threshold. What the heck? Why would a Mineheart ward keep us out? We were family, dang it. Well, at least I was.

Merlin looked back at us and his face grew even more solemn. "So that's it, is it? You're all here about Jack."

It took me a while, but my head finally wrapped around what was going on. The Mineheart wards worked by keeping out anyone with ill will towards someone inside the house. It was pretty obvious when you thought about it.

We'd just found Jack Watson. And after only

being on the case for less than a day. A new record for me.

Now, if only we could go in and get him.

Chapter 7

"It would appear we are at an impasse," Merlin said, his eyes boring into mine.

I nodded. "You do realize that you are harboring a criminal?"

He hesitated. "That might be true on the bigger side of things. However, he has told me that he is not guilty of this particular crime, and I believe him."

I had to chew that over for a minute. "If he's innocent, then you should be able to prove that in court, right? Isn't this something for them to decide rather than you? After all, you and Archie have a pretty good reputation for seeing justice done in court. What makes this time different?"

That got a frown. "My brother and I are very good at what we do, yes. And for the record, he is totally in the dark on this, and I'd appreciate it if that could stay that way."

Well yeah, he was risking a lot just having the

man in his home right now.

"You didn't answer my question."

Merlin took a deep breath. "This time I don't think I could save him. I'd be okay with that if he were guilty of the crime, but he isn't. I can't come to terms with him getting a hefty prison term for something he didn't do."

"But you admit he is a criminal."

"I do."

I stared at him. "And you do know that I could call the police in right now, and they would come and arrest him. It's not like he could run with us right here to take him down."

He tilted his head. "And you know that if the police are called in, it isn't just Jack they would arrest. I'd be going in a cell right along beside him. And the law firm that your father and I have spent our lives building would be ruined." He leaned toward me. "I just don't see the Amie I know and love doing that, do you?"

Crapsnackles. The man knew me too well.

Arc cleared his throat behind Merlin and all of us looked at him. "Um, guys I think we're missing the solution here. It might be more complicated, but I think Merlin and Jack would agree to let us turn him in if we can prove he's innocent. I mean, you have some experience with the whole investigation process, Amie. Even if you aren't licensed yet."

There goes an easy and simple case. Dang it. I'd really been counting on that payment for moving expenses.

"How much would you collect if you turned him over right this minute?"

I looked over at Ruby. She'd be the one to know that. I hadn't really looked at the numbers.

"A little over seventeen hundred dollars."

Enough to get us moved in, but the furniture

would probably have to wait. And we'd probably be doing the heavy lifting ourselves when it came down to it. But those rent a trucks weren't cheap, and we had three people's belongings to move.

"I'll write you a check for that right now." The voice wasn't one I recognized.

I leaned in as far as the ward would allow me to. The man standing off to the side was everything I'd expected him to be. Tall, handsome, the very image of a dapper thief. Talk about looking the part, he had it nailed. He even had a touch of a British accent too. Very Bond-ish.

"I take it you're Jack, huh?"

He nodded and smiled. "I'd offer my hand, but I'm half afraid you'd pull me through the doorway and take me away." He chuckled. "I'm afraid I don't have the trust in you that your uncle does."

"I'm sorry, but I don't think a check from you would go very far right now. Or do anything other than get us into more trouble than we need," Ruby said.

"Ah, yes. Hadn't thought of that."

"Then I'll cover it. Jack can pay me back once they drop the charges."

I still had reason to hesitate. "There's more to this job than the money."

"Crap, I'd forgotten about the deal," Arc said. "Vincent isn't going to let us work on any other cases until we bring Jack in." He looked at Merlin and Jack with a solemn face. "I'm starting to wish I'd never even seen that house. I don't want to cause trouble for Jack."

"You didn't cause my trouble, dear boy, but someone did. I swear upon my friendship with your family, something I treasure far more than anything else on earth, that I did not steal that necklace, nor do I have any idea how it came to be in my very own home."

Merlin grunted. "That wouldn't be the case if

you'd let me do a ward on your place like I wanted to."
Then he looked at me and Ruby. "I'm afraid old Jack
here doesn't believe in magic."

Jack chuckled. "What I really can't believe is
that you still insist that it exists. You might be able to do
some tricks, but I've seen many people on stage do
better ones, and they are no more witches than I am."

"Um, guys, could we maybe get back on target
here?" Arc asked. He looked over at me. "For what it's
worth, I'm with them. We either drop the case and walk
away, or we help them." He hesitated. "Well, actually
that isn't true. You two are welcome to walk away, and
maybe see if Ruby can negotiate another deal with
Vincent. But I'm staying on to help."

My brain was going double time. Personally, I
was having a hard time seeing why two men I trusted
were standing behind a known criminal just because he
was proclaiming his innocence. I mean, what was that
saying? The prisons are filled with innocent men? Just
ask them. But if Merlin and Arc were going to stand
firm, what more was there to do but join in?

"I vote we help," Ruby said. "We don't need all
that much money right now. And we have a whole year
to save up for that balloon payment. Even if we miss out
on Gray, there will be another one in due time."

Taking a deep breath, I nodded. And almost fell
into Merlin's house. I guess I'd been leaning a bit
against the ward. Silly me.

Merlin reached out and steadied me with a grin.
"That's more like the Amie I know and love." Then he
gathered me into a quick, but fierce, hug. "I'm so glad
you're finally part of the family."

Yeah, I kind of was too. Even if my new family
did come with its own set of problems. All families did.

Merlin led us through the house and out into an
enclosed back porch. The view was amazing. There was

actually a small creek running right through his backyard. If I didn't know any better, I'd say we were miles away from everything and not within easy walking distance of Oak Hill.

After getting us all drinks, Merlin nodded to Jack. "I know you've given me the gist of it, but you need to start from the beginning for these guys. Don't leave out anything. If they've agreed to help, you don't have to worry about them betraying you. You have my personal word that they won't."

Okay, that didn't put any pressure on or anything. But then, likely, that was his intention.

Jack leaned back. "Well, as I said, I didn't take the bloody necklace. However, if the police check, and I'm sure they will, my fingerprints will be in the mayor's house." He grimaced. "Which, if they stopped to think about it should point more toward my innocence than my guilt. I don't leave fingerprints when I'm working. It's unprofessional. Stupid, too."

"Why would they find your fingerprints at their house?" Ruby asked.

He gave her a kind look. "Because I was there." He shook his head. "A night I very much regret, actually, as I'm sure that's the night that will seal my doom on this one."

"But why were you there?" Ruby was being insistent. And as long as she was asking the same questions I'd be asking, I was more than okay with that. After all, she was kind of in training. I needed to see what kind of skills she had.

The silence grew.

"Because he was casing the place to actually rob them," Merlin said. "I told you, you can trust them, Jack. They aren't going to be able to help you if you don't tell them everything."

Jack sighed. "Very well. Yes, I was planning on

taking a few things at a later date. And the benefit they were holding was for a cause I support, so I went. I'm a big believer in the killing two birds with one stone theory." He paused. "My, I've never really thought about what a truly dreadful metaphor that is. But for the life of me, I can't think of a better one. I was using the benefit gathering as a prime opportunity to scope out the place."

"But you didn't take the necklace or anything else of value?" Sue me, I jumped in. Ruby just wasn't fast enough.

"I did not. If you don't count the food and drink that was freely offered."

"Okay," I said slowly, my brain wheels turning, "When was the necklace stolen? Do you have an alibi?" I was guessing not, or we wouldn't be here, but I had to ask.

"Sadly, they aren't sure exactly when the piece was stolen. Therefore, whether I actually have an alibi for the time of the theft or not is rather a moot point."

"So, the evidence against you amounts to them finding your prints at the scene of the crime and then finding the actual stolen necklace in your own home?" Arc shook his head. "Sounds pretty dang conclusive to me. How on earth are we going to prove you didn't do it?"

"Ah, therein lies the rub, I'm afraid."

"But if you didn't do it, then someone else did." Ruby was back in the game. "All we have to do is solve the original crime, and that will prove you didn't do it."

She had a point. Not that it would be easy when everyone else in the world would be convinced of Jack's guilt. Then I remembered that reporter. The one that gave himself a major out should Jack be proven innocent.

They all had a point. The more I thought about it, the more things just weren't adding up. So I backtracked.

"When the police came to your home, did they have a warrant?"

Jack shook his head. "No, they did not."

I leaned back. "Then it's inadmissible, right? An illegal search and seizure." Case closed.

"Not exactly," Merlin said, giving Jack a nasty look. "Jack gave them permission to enter and search, so the legality of their find stands, I'm afraid."

"Why the heck would you do that?" All three of us asked the same basic question at the exact same time. A few words may have varied here and there. I believe Arc's version of it had a bit stronger word than heck.

"He let them search without a warrant because he's far too cocky for his own good. And for once, it bit him in the butt," Merlin said, still glaring at Jack.

"In my defense, this isn't the first time I've done that, and they have never once found anything in my home that I've stolen. I'm far craftier than they are."

"Never until now, don't you mean?" Ruby asked.

He shook his head. "No, my statement stands as is. I did not steal that necklace. If I had, and then hidden it in the ridiculously easy to find spot they found it in, would I have invited them to search my home? No. I may be cocky, but I'm not stupid."

It was looking more and more like Jack really was innocent, which was a good thing, because we were all on this case, whether we wanted to be or not.

Chapter 8

We talked on for a little while longer at Merlin's and then left, still no closer to figuring out who might be the one that set up Jack to take the fall. Or, an even more important question, why. I mean, if a burglar went to the risk of stealing a piece of jewelry worth that much money, you'd think they'd want to keep it. Or exchange it for quick cash.

Taking the risk of that high-profile theft just to frame a known burglar? It just didn't make sense.

All of us agreed to look into it and to meet back in the middle of the week at Merlin's to discuss what we found, or didn't find. Hopefully, by then, I'd have some kind of clue or, at the very least, a theory. Those came best to me while I was occupied with other things.

Like moving.

The inspection report had come back with no surprises, the paperwork was finalized, and the owner had offered us immediate possession. There was nothing standing in our way from moving in right away. I was elated and scared silly all at the same time.

The only home I'd ever had was the farmhouse. I loved my tiny little apartment. The thought of it not being there waiting for me if things didn't work out was really bothering me. That part of things had hit me kind of hard.

So be it. Maybe it was just the Goddess' way of telling me it was time to fly the coop and not look back.

We stopped by the market and picked up as many boxes as they had, then stopped a few other places and gathered more. It wasn't like we had tons of stuff to move. Ruby and I weren't really hoarders of things. Bedroom furniture, a small table and chairs, and a couch and chair were pretty much it for me. At least for the heavy lifting part of things we'd need a truck or van for.

Our plan was to rent a truck the following Friday. Until then, we'd be packing things up and moving boxes back and forth. It would be a hard week. All the better to let the problem of Jack stew until I came up with something brilliant, right?

By the middle of the following day, I had pretty much filled up my share of the boxes we'd gathered. I stood looking at them and made a decision.

We each had keys to both of our respective houses. I was going to load everything in my car, drive it over, and unpack. If I unpacked as I went, it wouldn't be nearly as hard as doing it all at once. Plus, that would free up the boxes to use again. Win-win.

I was kind of disappointed when I pulled in and saw Arc's car sitting in the driveway. I'd thought he and Ruby would both be at work. After all, it was Monday, and they both had jobs during the week.

I'd really been hoping to have the place all to myself to explore. It was one thing being there with everyone else, but I wanted some alone time with my new home. Didn't look like I would get it today, though.

The sound of my car must have alerted Ruby because she stepped out onto the porch. Of my house. Sue me for being a little territorial, but she had her own place, didn't she? Shouldn't that be where I'd find her?

"Shouldn't you be at work?" I asked as I stepped onto the porch beside her.

She nodded. "Totally should be, but Mom said I was making too many mistakes, so I should just give it up and come out here and start the moving in process." She paused. "She wasn't wrong. I couldn't keep my mind off things here. Too excited, I guess."

I could understand that. The excitement bug had definitely taken a bite out of me too.

"Is Arc here too?" I was proud of myself. I'd asked two questions so far and neither one of them was 'why were you in my house?'.

"Nope, just me." She blushed. "I was trying to surprise you, but you caught me. Come on in, and I'll show you."

Goddess, but I hated when people tried to surprise me. But I smiled and nodded and followed her in.

The house was just as empty as I remembered it until we got to the kitchen.

"Mom bought a couple of storage units in an auction to see if there would be anything inside worthy of the shop. One of them held a lot of kitchen stuff. Not really the stuff she's into for the shop, so she gave the boxes to me." She waved over at the boxes sitting on just about every available surface of the room. "And I decided to share."

I just looked at her. "You mean there's more?"

"Oh yeah, a lot more. This isn't even half. I tried to keep the duplicates to a minimum. But Mom knows we didn't keep a lot of kitchen stuff in our apartments. I think this is her way of helping us get started. I hoped to have everything lined out for you before you got here."

Okay, so that was nice of her. And instantly I felt guilty about the whole territorial thing. I should have known better. I mean, it was Ruby, right? If I didn't trust her, I wouldn't have given her a key, now would I? And if she didn't trust me, there wouldn't be a barn key on my ring too.

It was a cousin kind of thing.

The boxes held a wonderful bounty. Enough to almost make me wish I was a little better in the kitchen. Or maybe a lot better.

But with all this stuff, I now had the tools I needed to learn. The bigger items included a crockpot, an air fryer, and a full set of expensive cookware with copper bottoms. To buy all this stuff at retail cost would cost a fortune. Opal had to have paid a pretty penny for all this. And while it might not have been her shop's usual kind of fare, she still could have sold it. It was nice of her to think of us instead.

We tried to order pizza delivered, but ran into a stumbling block. It would appear that the convenience of having ready-made food delivered to your door was a town kind of thing. Here is the country, things worked a little differently. If you wanted food out here, you either made it yourself or you went to get it.

While we now had the utensils to make our own food, we didn't have any actual food to use them on. So, we drove to Oak Hill. The selection of restaurants was better there. We even decided to be nice and invite Arç to join us.

After lunch, we were right back at it. By the early evening, we had not just my kitchen up and ready for business, but Ruby's as well. It had turned out to be a very productive day.

"I say we stay here tonight."

I just looked at her. "You do know that we won't have our beds until this weekend, right?" Sleeping on the floor wasn't all that appealing to me.

"Yeah, but we have our yoga mats. We could use them under our sleeping bags. And we have electricity and heat, so there really isn't anything to stop us."

Well, except for the lack of furniture. But it would be really nice to have one solid night's sleep without being woken up by a baby's cry. Little Pearl was a good baby. Normally she only woke up the one time now for her midnight feeding, but still. A full night of heavenly peace and quiet was extremely tempting.

It wasn't as if they needed me at the farmhouse. Between Kimberly, Opal, and Nancy, the baby was well taken care of.

"Okay, I'm in. But we need to make a stop at the store before settling in." A yoga mat might help, but I was thinking more along the lines of a full-blown (pardon the pun) air mattress. All the comfort of home even without a bed.

"No problem. I have to go pick up Arc from work, anyway. I kind of figured I'd stop off and pick up a few groceries and drinks and stuff to do us for a few days while we do our thing here. But I was kind of thinking of grabbing something out to eat tonight. I know our kitchens are ready to use but..."

But after a hard day's work setting up not one but two kitchens, we needed a break. Having the kitchens ready to go was a really nice feeling. Having to use them to make a meal, plus the clean up afterward? Not so much.

"How does Carney's sound?" Like I had to ask. "While you head to pick up Arc, I'm going to hit the store for a few things and then go to the farmhouse to grab more boxes. The more I can bring over and empty out, the more I have to refill tomorrow."

She nodded. "That's not a bad idea. I might join you doing that tomorrow. If Mom agrees to give me another day off." She looked around. "Unpacking won't be nearly as much fun without you being there beside me though."

Ruby grew quiet. I knew what she was thinking. I was thinking it too. It would be super weird not living under the same roof. I was just hoping that having her on the same property would help that. We'd find out soon enough.

My errands didn't take long. I picked up a full-sized air mattress for me and a queen-sized one for Arc and Ruby. It was the least I could do. But I saved the receipts just in case she had the same idea I did when it came to a comfortable sleeping arrangement for the night.

Then I loaded down the car. Almost to capacity. I was saving the front passenger seat. I was hoping I could use the lure of Carney's and good company to get Opie to join us for the night. The sooner he fell in love with the place, the better. I really hoped I wouldn't be living alone in that big house for long.

Unfortunately, as it turned out, he had other plans. Ones I wasn't totally sure I was okay with.

Chapter 9

I called first to make sure he was home. He was, so I swung by his apartment and even carried in a pizza. How could he get the tempting smell otherwise?

It kind of shocked me to find him packing.

"You skipping out without telling your girlfriend? That's not cool, just so you know."

He smiled up at me. "I was just getting ready to call you when you called me." He crossed the room to me, taking a big whiff of the pizza. "Is that for me? I knew there was a reason I loved you."

I pulled the box out of his reach. "Not until I know what the bags are all about. I was kind of hoping that you'd join me, Ruby, and Arc tonight. We're going to camp out for our first night at the new house." And I really, really want you to start seeing it as a home too. But that, I didn't say out loud.

He grimaced. "Sorry, I'm going to have to miss it. Dad got a call from Giovanni Rosati. It seems he's decided to elope and wants me and Dad to take care of the security for him. Hopefully, we'll be able to keep everyone alive at this wedding."

Yeah, that hadn't turned out to be the case at the last Rosati wedding. But then again, the murder had happened before Opie and the sheriff got settled in. Totally not their fault.

Security is a big deal when the Michigan mob boss is involved. And that's exactly what Giovanni Rosati is. He's also, believe it or not, a decent and caring human being. Oh, and he's a witch too.

"Van's getting married? When the heck did that happen? Last I knew he was a very happy widower." Then it hit me. "Wait a minute. Van's getting married, and he hasn't asked me to come and do the wedding photos? I think I'm insulted."

Opie blushed and then scrubbed at his chin. "Oh, he wanted to get you, but the bride to be kind of put a nix to that."

I just looked at him. "The bride has an issue with me?" I mean, I knew Van, and I liked him, even if he was the Mob boss of Michigan. But there had never been anything like a romantic relationship between the two of us.

He nodded. "Yeah, she kind of does. Something about you taking her down in a cage fight and then making her tap out."

I almost dropped the pizza. Would have, if Opie hadn't been ready for it.

"Van's marrying Missy Daniels?"

"Yup. He met her the last time he came down to visit Dad. I guess it was love at first sight."

More like she saw an opportunity to never have to work another day in her life. Van wasn't a poor man by any means. I really didn't like Missy much.

"So, you're telling me that you are leaving me to

work security for Missy Daniel's wedding?"

He took a deep breath and shook his head. "No. And I'm not leaving you. I'll only be gone three or four days tops. I'm hoping to be back for the big move-in to help out with the heavy lifting. And I'm not working security for Missy. I'm helping Dad with security for Van." He looked me in the eyes. "You know that."

Did I? A part of me still didn't like it. I felt sorry for Van, but it would be super nice to have Missy off the singles market. And out of Wind's Crossing. I really didn't trust her around Opie. She'd made a play for him before.

He sat the pizza down and gathered me into a hug. I would miss this. Even if it was only for a few days.

"Promise me you'll stay out of trouble while I'm gone?"

I gave a half-hearted shrug. "I promise I'll try, but you know trouble has a habit of finding me wherever I go." I laid my ear up against his chest and listened to his heart beating. "Promise me you'll be safe? If someone dies at this wedding, it better not be you, got it?"

"I'll be just as safe as I can be. And I'll have Dad to watch my back." He grew quiet. "The whole Missy thing isn't going to cause problems with us again, is it? Maybe I should call Dad…"

I took a stuttered breath and pulled away. "No. I trust you. And your dad needs someone he can trust there to watch his back too. No one fits that description better than you."

He leaned down, his chin resting on the top of my head. "So, we're good here?"

"Yeah, we're good. Just don't let me live to regret letting you go."

"And do I get to keep the pizza?"

***

It would mean only having one extra-large pizza to share between three people, but I let him keep it. Call me a fool for love.

Come to find out, Ruby hadn't thought about getting an air mattress, either. Both she and Arc were thrilled with my little present to them when we all met back up. So much so that Arc carried in all my boxes and even took them up the stairs and into the room I'd chosen as my bedroom.

It was kind of nice, this having a brother thing. Muscles and all.

Once the boxes were in and the mattresses all laid out ready for filling, we dug into the pizza. We'd resisted the alluring temptation of the smell long enough. So what if our beds for the night would be filled with a garlicky goodness smell?

"I don't suppose you thought to get an electric air pump?" Arc asked, eyeing the now flat mattresses as he munched.

"They have those?" Crap. I wish I'd known that while I was at the store. Ah well, there were three of us, and we had time before bedtime to get them filled up. Couldn't take all that much, could it?

He shook his head but didn't say anything. So I decided to fill the conversation gap.

I'd felt a little guilty spending the entire day doing personal errands when we'd agreed to help Jack with his problem. The problem was, I had absolutely no idea where to start.

"I don't suppose either of you has made any kind of breakthrough on the case we took on?"

Ruby shook her head, but Arc looked thoughtful.

"Well, I wouldn't exactly call it a breakthrough,

but I do have an idea about it," Arc said.

"Are you waiting for an invitation?" Ruby asked. "Spill, already."

He grinned. Arc's my brother, and I love him, but he can be a bit of a jerk at times.

"Well, since you asked so nicely," he said. "I was just wondering how the necklace got into Jack's house. I've been to his house. As a criminal himself, he takes his home security very seriously. I'm thinking it has to be another burglar. A very good one at that."

"Didn't your family ever set up wards for him?" Ruby asked. "If he and Merlin are all that close, you would think they would have."

He shrugged. "We totally would have, but Jack said no. Merlin wasn't kidding when he said Jack didn't believe in magic."

"His loss." But Arc had a very good point. Whoever planted that evidence had to first steal it from the Mayor's wife and then go so far as to break into Jack's and plant it there. Somewhere the police would be sure to look. Sounded like a burglar to me too.

"Where does that leave us? Did you ask Jack if maybe someone in his field had it out for him?"

Arc nodded. "I did." He took another bite of pizza and started chewing.

It was getting on my nerves. "You know, this would go a whole heck of a lot faster if you would just stop with all the theatrics and tell us what you learned. We're a team now, remember? The sooner we put this to rest, the sooner we can start making real money."

At least he had the grace to look embarrassed. "Sorry. I'm kind of new to the whole team thing." He swallowed the last of the bite and then started again. "According to Jack, there is a whole group of burglars that work through a kind of broker. The broker makes the deals for the jobs and then posts them in a coded advertisement in the paper. Each group member has their own code. It seems that Jack has kind of been the favorite, getting a lot of the higher paying gigs. He said he wouldn't put it past any of the others to try to put him away."

"And he didn't think to mention this last night?" Seemed pretty important to me.

Another shrug. "He says he doesn't really think knowing that will help us all that much." He hesitated, then thought of himself when I narrowed my eyes at him. "He says that none of them know anything about the others. He's clueless as to who they all are."

"Does the broker know?" Ruby asked.

"Whether they know or not is kind of a moot point. Jack doesn't know who the broker is either."

Ruby and I looked at each other.

"Then how on earth did they set up such an elaborate system?" I asked. Someone had to know something.

"He can't speak for the others, but Jack got a package delivered to his doorstep. At first, he thought it was a joke, but it wasn't. He says the broker is great at handling the day-to-day stuff of finding and assigning jobs. Leaves him and the others to concentrate on what they do best."

Sounded like we would have to try our hand at code breaking.

"But wait a minute," Ruby said, holding one hand up. "If none of them know who the others are, then how did the burglar know about Jack?"

Crapsnackles.

We were right back to square one.

***

We decided to all have a group camp out of sorts in the downstairs living room. I was kind of grateful, actually. Spending the first night in a new place isn't nearly as scary when you're surrounded by family. Luckily, they seemed to think the same way.

"You guys promise to be good, right?" I asked.

Arc raised his eyebrows. "Of course. But, come on, what could we possibly do that would be so very terrible? Put your bra in the freezer? Girls do that kind of thing at slumber parties, don't they?"

I didn't like the thoughtful look on his face right then. "Not ones that don't want hexes placed on them."

He nodded. "Point taken."

Ruby punched his arm. "She was talking about bedroom activities, silly. She doesn't want us getting all hot and bothered with her in the same room."

The color rose in his cheeks. "Come on now! We're not rabbits!"

Ruby gave me a wink. "Well, sometimes we're a little bunny like."

He turned away and headed for the front door. "I'm going out for a walk."

We waited until the door closed behind him before laughing. It wasn't easy. He was fun to play with sometimes.

I looked over at the mattresses still lying flat and airless on the floor. "We should probably get started on blowing those up, huh?"

Ruby's gaze went to them too. "Yeah, we should." Then there was silence as neither of us moved. "But you know, I'm thinking those boxes Arc carried upstairs for you might be a better way to spend the time. How about you?"

We were so alike. "Absolutely. What are the chances we could get Arc to blow them up for us?"

"Probably would have been better before the whole rabbit discussion."

"Yeah, that's what I think too."

"Maybe I'll go and try to unruffle his feathers a bit." She gave me a sly smile. "Don't come looking for us for at least an hour, okay?"

Now the blushing bug caught on. "I'll just wait here for you two to come back." No way would I be looking for them anytime soon.

After she left, I gathered the paper plates and utensils and shoved all the trash in a bag. Then I placed the bag under the sink. First thing tomorrow I'd have to bring over a trash can. Moving in was bound to create a lot of trash. Wouldn't hurt to call and arrange for the local trash pickup too. That kind of stuff could accumulate pretty quickly.

Then I took a deep breath and headed up the stairs. Yes, sorting out my boxes of clothes was better than puffing endlessly into an air mattress. But not by all that great much. I'd still need the boxes tomorrow, though, so it was a job that needed to be done.

My plan was to hang up everything I could hang and then make neat little stacks of all my foldables. Of course, the best-laid plans sometimes go astray.

Like mine did when I crossed the threshold into my bedroom and found it already occupied.

Chapter 10

I'm not totally sure, but I think I might have screamed a little. Not that the woman going through my things was all that scary, but she caught me by surprise. What the heck was she doing in my house? And just how long had she been up here?

"What in the blazes do you think you're doing?"

She whirled around to face me and recognition set in. It was the same woman that had been with the owner the day we came to look at the house. Surely she had to know that the house was no longer his, right? I mean it would really bite if he didn't tell her something like that.

Her face was a picture of confusion and wonder as she tilted her head and gazed at me. Then she looked behind herself at the wall. And then back at me.

"You can see me?" she whispered.

What the hell? "Of course, I can see you, you're standing right bloody in front of me! I'm not blind."

She blinked at me and then her eyes lit up like a kid on Christmas morning. "You can really see me? And hear me too?"

I opened my mouth to answer her but stopped when I heard footsteps pounding up the stairs. The others must have heard my scream.

Arc burst through the doorway. "What is it? What's wrong? Are you all right?"

Then he looked behind me and saw the woman. "Who the hell is that?"

The woman started bouncing on her heels. "You can see me too? Oh, this is wonderful!"

"Of course, I can see you. You're standing right there in front of us."

"That's exactly what I said."

Then Ruby burst in, breathless from the short run. "We heard you scream, are you—who the heck is she?"

I waited for the woman to ask if Ruby could see her too, but she didn't. Twice must have been enough. Even for her.

"You mean the invisible woman?" I asked. "She seems to think we shouldn't be able to see her."

"Invisible? What the heck are you talking about?" Ruby asked. "She's standing right there."

"That's what we keep telling her. But right now, you know as much as I do."

"How long has she been here? I sure as heck didn't see her come in. Did you?" Ruby asked. After all, we'd been there most of the day.

I shook my head, then turned to the woman. "Now that we've established our ability to see you, would you mind answering us? Who the heck are you and what are you doing here going through my stuff?"

She ducked her head. "Sorry, if I invaded your privacy going through your stuff. I get bored. When new people come, it's fun for a while. Something different finally." She turned away briefly. "At least until the frustration kicks back in."

Then she turned back to us, and I'd swear she was glowing. I mean really glowing. People didn't normally do that. Did they?

"But look at me now. I mean, it isn't just that you can see me, you're actually talking to me! How awesome is that?"

I was starting to worry about her sanity. It might be time to call the sheriff. And maybe the guy that had sold us this place. There was definitely something he'd forgotten to mention.

"Um, Amie?" Ruby's voice cracked a little, but I was far too concerned with the woman in front of me to really pay much attention to that.

"In a minute, Ruby," I said, my eyes not wavering from the woman. "Did the guy that owns this place not tell you that he sold it? We aren't just 'new people', we're the new owners. You're going to need to leave."

"Uh, Amie?" Ruby was being annoying persistent. Couldn't she tell I was a little busy at the moment?

"Hold on, Ruby." I was dealing with a major problem here.

The woman gave me a sad look. "I can't do that."

My heart went out to her, but there had to be someplace she could go. Family, friends, even a shelter if need be. I wasn't at all sure I'd be comfortable with a woman missing a few marbles sleeping in the same house as me. Who knew what she might be capable of?

"We'll help you find a place to stay tonight, if that's what you're worried about," I told her. "But you need to leave." I glanced over at Arc. "Do you have that guy's address? I think maybe we need to take her to him and let him deal with this."

When Arc didn't immediately answer, I turned to him. He and Ruby were standing frozen in their shoes staring at the woman.

"What?"

Ruby swallowed. "Amie, I think you need to take a really good look at her," she whispered. Her voice was definitely cracking. "And, like, maybe the wall directly behind her too?"

Frowning I turned again to the woman. She was still giving me that sad look. I started to wonder what the heck it was that everyone else knew that I didn't.

Then I saw it. The wall. Directly behind her, just like Ruby said. Seeing the wall might not be an issue on a normal basis. But I was seeing the wall through the woman's body. Barely, but if I concentrated, I could definitely see the wall.

What the bloody hell?

"As I was saying," she said. "I can't leave." She waved her arms around her. "This is my home, and apparently I'm not allowed off my property. Kind of annoying, as the only enjoyment I was getting out of my death was making my worthless brother's life miserable. Now he's gone, and I'm stuck here." She gave me a timid smile. "I really hope you guys stay. I'll be good, I promise. Please stay?"

I stared at her. "You're a… a…"

"Ghost. And yes, it would appear so."

"Hey, guys," Arc said, his voice full of wonder. "We just bought a haunted house. How cool is that?"

Cool? I could think of a lot of words to describe what it was, all right, but cool was not one of them. He might think differently if she was haunting their barn instead of the house.

Wait a minute. She hadn't said she couldn't leave the house. She'd said distinctly that she couldn't leave the property. I know it shouldn't have, but that thought actually gave me a lot of comfort at the moment.

The woman grinned at Arc. "I'm glad you think so. The past people Kyle has tried to pawn the house and me off on haven't been all that happy about it." Then she looked at me. "I would say that I'm sorry you were misled into buying the house, but the truth is, I'm thrilled. You don't know what it's like going years without talking to someone."

She grew pensive. "Well, that's not entirely true. I could talk. It's just that nobody could hear me. That gets really boring after a while. Kind of makes me sad that I was such a hermit in life. I really didn't know how much human interaction means to a person."

Well, at least I didn't think she was crazy anymore. That was something, right? A small step up?

I mean, how freaky would it be trying to sleep in a house haunted by a crazy woman, right? Haunted by a sane woman was bad enough.

"Are there any more ghosts we should know about?" I asked. Funny, my voice cracked just a bit too. It must be catching.

She shook her head. "Just me. I don't even have one of them to talk to. It's been lonely the past few years." She paused. "At least I think it's been years. Kind of hard to tell without access to calendars and such." Her eyes darkened. "It didn't help when my jerk brother moved out all my stuff either."

I thought about the near-perfect little library. The one room that had more than sold me on the house itself. "He didn't take all of it though, did he?"

She grinned at me. "Oh, he tried. I'm kind of limited on how much energy I can spend in a day, so I concentrated it on my library. It always was my favorite room in the house."

Well, what did you know? I had something in common with a ghost.

Chapter 11

Come to find out, staying in a haunted house really wasn't all that bad once you got to know the ghost. We spent the rest of the night together down in the living room. Liz even joined us for most of it.

That was her name. Liz. Liz Jordan. If we had wanted juicy stories of murder and mayhem—which I, for one, most decidedly did not—we would have been disappointed. According to Liz she apparently tripped and fell down the stairs in the middle of the night. They had ruled her death accidental, as she'd been alone in the house at the time.

"Did you trip on something?" Ruby asked, leaning in. She was really getting into the whole talking with a ghost thing.

Liz shrugged. "I really don't know what happened at all. I can't remember a thing from that night. I'm thinking maybe the powers that be don't want us ghosts running around remembering all the grisly details. At least that's all I can figure about it. I remember going to bed that night, and then… well, nothing until I basically woke up dead."

"Wasn't there a light you were supposed to go into?" Arc asked. "I mean all the near-death experiences I've heard of said there was a light."

She shook her head. "They must not have paid the heavenly electric bill or something, because I didn't get any light." She shivered. "At least I didn't get the other place either."

Ruby looked over at me. "Did you think you might?"

Liz thought for a minute. "No. I'm… okay, I was, a decent person. I just kept to myself a lot. I didn't go out of my way to hurt anyone." She hesitated. "But I didn't really go out of my way to help anyone either. Maybe that's why I had to stick around here. Some kind of limbo until I prove myself one way or the other? Only I don't have a clue how I'm supposed to do that when I'm stuck here."

"So all you do all day, every day is just hang around here?" Man, did that sound sad. "Good thing you stocked up your library with books, then, huh?"

All that got me was a sad look. "It would have been. If I could actually pick one up and open it."

Wow. All those books right there and not being able to read a single one of them? That had to be pure torture. My heart really did go out to her now. No wonder she'd been so excited when we could see her. Which reminded me.

"Do you have any idea why no one else could see or hear you? I mean, you said you made your brother's life miserable. How did you manage to do that?"

She gave me a rather evil smile. "Oh, there are ways. I can't really move things, but I can do smaller things that eventually add up. Temperature is a big one I can control. Let's just say, he was never warm in the house. Plus, sometimes, if I concentrate really hard, I can create a breeze. Enough to knock something off a shelf and stuff like that. I can't touch things directly, but the breeze can."

That kind of made sense.

Eventually, even as awesome as it was talking with one of the dearly departed, we had to call it a night. We had managed, during lulls in the conversation, to actually get the beds blown up. When we started to lie down, Liz started toward the stairs.

I could tell she didn't really want to go. "You can stay down here with us if you like. As long as you don't freeze us out."

She giggled. "I wouldn't do that. I like you."

"What did your brother do that made you dislike him so much?" Arc asked. Hopefully, he'd be taking notes of things not to do with me. I have to admit, even though I love Arc, haunting him would be something I could totally see myself doing.

"No one thing. Just who he was really." She shivered. "He isn't a nice person. If he made out the contract you signed for this place, I really hope you ran it through an attorney first."

"We did. Everything seemed to be in place and Dad fixed what wasn't."

"Good. He's known for taking advantage of things like that. He was really jealous of my place here. I never intended for it to go to him, but at twenty-five, you really don't think about dying, so I didn't have a will in place. And the jerk is my closest next of kin, so everything I worked so hard for went to him."

"That's pretty crappy," Ruby said. "I totally get why you would haunt him. Too bad you couldn't follow him though."

"Yeah. But then again, if I'd followed him, I might not have met you guys. It's nice to have friends again." Then she stopped. "At least I hope we'll be friends."

I looked at the others. From what I could read on their faces, that would not be a problem.

I knew it sure as heck wasn't a problem for me.

But I did kind of wonder how Opie would take the news.

***

The next morning, we all managed to get up in time to see the worker-bees off to their daily jobs. They might not have gotten the full eight hours of prescribed sleep, but that didn't stop them from going off, anyway.

Unfortunately, that kind of meant I had to get up and go too. Arc worked in Oak Hill and Ruby worked in Wind's Crossing. I could have let Ruby borrow my car, but I didn't think Destiny would be too happy with me if I didn't come home today.

And if there's one thing I've learned in life, it's that you don't want to piss off a Goddess kitten.

There was no sign of Liz, but before I left, I went upstairs and pulled a couple of random books off the shelves. I couldn't come up with a way for her to turn the pages, but at least she could have a few minutes' enjoyment out of the open books. I planned to make sure I got my television set on one of today's loads too. Not that television was all that entertaining at the best of times, but it beat staring at the walls of an empty house all day.

We weren't going to make it to the farmhouse before Opal and Kimberly left for the shop, so we stopped at the shop first. Opal had rigged a small corner of the back of the shop into a kind of nursery, complete with a crib and baby toys. The children went to work with them, and one of them made sure that the older kids made it to and from school on time.

It was kind of hard to imagine a time when Kimberly hadn't been a part of our lives. She fit with us so very well. The baby was new, as was having kids in the house, but it was a nice kind of new. Even if I did miss my privacy, I'd be missing them even more once my move into the house was final.

With the stop, and the subsequent visiting time, it was after ten when I finally made it to Destiny. She was not amused.

I walked in to find her on the back of my sofa facing away from the door. Any other time, she met me as I walked in. Not today. This would be touch and go. Lucky for me, I had a secret weapon.

"I know you're probably mad at me for not taking you with me last night, but I have big news to share. And I'm willing to share it over an egg and bacon omelet if you're interested."

Her ears twitched, but no true movement elsewhere.

I opened the bag from the restaurant and let the aroma of the food spread a little more. "Man, that smells good, doesn't it?"

The tiny feline head finally turned slowly toward me. "I should have been there. I could have helped."

My eyebrow raised. Of course, it stood to reason that Destiny would have already known about the house's occupant. The question was, why had she not thought it important enough to tell me about it?

Now she turned fully toward me, looking as smug as it was possible for a cat to look. "Well, according to our agreement, I'm limited in the times I can talk to you, aren't I?"

I should have known that would come back to

bite me on the heiny.

"I believe the deal was that you only used the ability to… whatever the heck this is… when I came to you or if there was something important that you needed to tell me. Personally, I think telling someone that the house they are buying is haunted would qualify as important."

She lifted a little kitty shoulder. Who knew cats could shrug? "It's not like she puts you in any kind of danger now, is it? She's a Casper of ghosts, not one of the Boo Brothers." She lifted a paw to give it a dainty lick. "Besides, everyone needs a few surprises in life. I just wanted to be there for it, that's all."

Now I was getting the full picture. She'd had no intention of ever telling me. The only thing upsetting her was that she'd missed the show.

It was almost enough for me to eat the entire omelet and not share. But I'm not quite that stupid.

We ate and then went to gather Yorkie Doodle from downstairs for a short walk. That was Destiny's suggestion. She seemed to think we were ignoring our familiars in all the excitement of moving. It's not like I could really say she was wrong.

So, we all went for a nice walk up the hill to the bonfire site, and I gathered some spell ingredients along the way. It wouldn't do to waste a nice walk in the woods. Besides, Opal's stock had to be getting low. I'd make sure to drop these by the shop on my next run to the house.

As we made our way back down the hill, I looked down at Destiny. "So, you know I will be splitting my time between the farmhouse and the new place for the next week or so. And I know you aren't overly fond of car rides, so what do you suggest? Do you want to stay here or go to the new place a little early?" I paused. "I really think you'd be more comfortable here, you know. There isn't any furniture at the new place. No soft, cushy places to lay."

She gazed up at me. "It's about time you asked me." Destiny looked over at Yorkie Doodle and they shared a look. "And how hard would be it be to bring my cat bed and Yorkie's dog mat? In fact, we'd much prefer riding in the car on them than being stuffed into that kennel thing you always insist on. It's not like we're going to interfere with your driving or anything."

Destiny was talking now for Yorkie Doodle too? Of course, she was. Why on earth should I be surprised by that?

I nodded. "Okay, so you guys are going to the new place then?" I looked down at Yorkie. "Will you be okay there too? As I said, it's bare-bones right now."

He gave a small yip. I had to wonder if Destiny had shared the whole bark means yes, tail wag means no thing with him. Right now, I was guessing the answer to that was Woof.

Chapter 12

I'd left my cell phone on the table in my apartment. When we got back from our little jaunt through the woods, I found that I'd missed a call.

From Lily. That was super odd. I knew it was her number because we'd all put it into our phones in case of emergency, but I couldn't recall her ever actually calling me. Not since the whole Arc frame-up thing, anyway. But there it was. A missed call from Lily.

I hit the redial to call her, and she answered on the first ring.

"Hey, Lily, is everything okay?" I know I can be a negative person, but somehow that's where my mind leaps in times like these.

"Everything is fine, dear. I was just talking to Merlin, and he said you three kids are staying at the house already."

I released the breath I'd been holding. All was good. "Yeah, we kind of camped out there last night." I hesitated about telling her about Liz. After all, I wasn't sure if she'd actually believe me. I know for a fact that up until last night, I'd thought ghosts didn't exist. Meeting a spirit in person, though, can really change one's mind on that.

In the end, I kept my mouth shut. Better to let the others find out on their own. Maybe by meeting her themselves.

"Well, in my younger days, I might have done the same thing. Getting your first place is exciting, I know. But it can be uncomfortable without a bed to sleep in."

Tell me about it. My mattress had held up decently for most of the night, but by morning I was pretty much on the floor again. And if we brought over Destiny and Yorkie, well, claws and air mattresses probably weren't a good combination.

"That's true." What more was there to say?

"Well, I'm free today. I wanted to offer my time and the use of my van to at least get your beds in and set up. We'd have to make three trips, one for each bed, so it would probably be an all-day job. But at least tonight, you would all have beds." She paused. "Unless you had other plans today?"

I hesitated. I did have plans to work on Jack's case today. But then again, he was safely hidden away at Merlin's, and right now the money wasn't such a pressing issue. Especially since Merlin had fronted the money we'd have made for the bounty. He'd get it back, of course, once we solved the riddle and turned Jack over.

That was our whole plan. Figure out who framed him, turn him in and collect the bond payment, then have Merlin present the evidence to the court, and thusly prove Jack's innocence. Our plan might not have a lot of details, but at least we had one.

But weighing starting on the case versus having my own bed to sleep in? Sorry, Jack.

"Nothing that can't wait until tomorrow. If you're sure you don't mind, I'd love to take you up on the offer."

"Wonderful, dear. We'll start with you girl's beds." There was a moment of silence. "Actually, I'm being a bit dense, aren't I? Arc and Ruby really wouldn't need two beds at the moment, would they?"

"Funny, but you're right. I didn't think about that either. So, we'll only have two trips. And actually, if we could just get the mattresses, we might even make it in one."

"We'll see, dear. When can you be ready to start?"

I glanced around. I'd already feed the critters and even taken them for a nice walk. I was as ready as I'd ever be. "Anytime would be fine by me."

"Good, because I'm just about ready to pull into your drive. See you in a minute."

I glanced out the window and sure enough, Lily's van came wheeling into the driveway. She had to have known we wouldn't turn her down. Though I am a bit surprised she didn't call before she left Oak Hill. That would have been a long drive to make if I hadn't been home.

Then again, there was always Ruby and Opal at the shop. Still a puzzle though.

As I opened the door at the bottom of the stairs for her, she gave me a smile and stepped through.

"So sorry for not calling first, dear. Or, well, not calling earlier," she said. "Did I catch you at a bad time?"

I glanced down at myself. I looked a bit wrinkled. I was still in the clothes from yesterday, and most likely I needed a shower in the worst way. We'd tried to get every minute of sleep this morning we could, so by the time we had gotten up, there hadn't been a lot of time to spare for the niceties of life.

It would probably be rude to sniff my armpit in front of her. Although I had to physically stop myself from doing so all the same.

Her smile deepened. "I know you probably didn't have time to shower this morning, dear. Nothing to be ashamed of." She glanced up the stairs towards my apartment. "If you want, I could start tearing down your bed while you take one. The hard part will be loading everything in the van."

Especially considering the stairs. Good thing my bed was just a full-sized and not a Queen or King. Then I remembered the kid's cardboard slide thing. It was worth a shot.

My shower only took a matter of maybe five minutes, and that included getting undressed and redressed. But when I came out, my bed was already dismantled and sitting there waiting to be carried down.

"Wow. You're really good at this."

Lily grinned. "I've had a lot more years than you have to practice." She lifted a small, but apparently mighty, hammer. "When you have the right tools, it doesn't take long."

I'd have to take her word for it. I still remember how long it took me and Ruby to dismantle that bed when I moved across the hall a few years ago.

It was a whole lot longer than five minutes.

***

We were halfway to the new place—we really needed to give it a name—when I began to suspect that just maybe Lily had an ulterior motive for helping me out today.

"So, I hear you and the others have agreed to

help out Jack Watson."

Oh yeah, with her and Merlin being so close, and Jack and Merlin being so close, it was only reasonable to think that just maybe she and Jack might be close too.

"Are you close to him too?"

She nodded. "Oh yes. The three of us went to high school together, you know. Fast friends all the way through." She chuckled. "I have to admit Merlin and I used to have some fun with him. What with his total disbelief in magic of any kind. We tried at first to convince him otherwise, then just gave up and had fun with it."

I could see that. Kind of made me feel sorry for the teenage Jack Watson, though.

"What did you do to him?"

"Nothing major, of course, like I said we were all friends. Just little things that really couldn't be explained any other way than magic." She paused. "Or so we thought. Jack always found a way. He's very resourceful."

After chewing my lip for a minute, I had to ask. "Do you think he really is innocent this time?"

Her grin was gone. "I'm absolutely one hundred percent sure of it. Jack doesn't lie to us. Besides, he's far too clever to let the police search his home when he has a stolen necklace sitting in the pocket of his jacket."

"That's where they found it then? In his pocket?" She was right, that didn't sound convincing at all. "Surely the police had to know that was a bit too easy, didn't they?"

"Apparently not. And the judge he's set to go up in front of isn't one to take repetitive crimes lightly. If he's found guilty on this one, he'll be sent up for quite a long stretch. And the three of us aren't getting any younger, you know."

"I don't suppose you have any kind of information that could help us prove that, do you?"

She hesitated. It was slight, and I almost missed it, but it was there.

"I'm sorry, but no, I don't. You're all on your own on this one I'm afraid."

Oh, I was afraid of that all right.

"Okay, let's go another way. You know Jack really well. Do you know anyone that would want to hurt him?"

Lily tilted her head and thought for a minute. "Well, a couple of things come to mind, now that I really think about it. One is that Jack has done some time—small sentences, thanks to Merlin—for other burglaries. And not all of his victims got all of their stuff back. There could be some ticked off people out there thinking that maybe he should do more time."

That made sense. "I don't suppose you have a list of all his past victims?"

The hesitation was longer this time. I had the feeling that Lily was hiding something from me. But surely if she knew something that would help out an old friend, she'd just come out with it, right?

"Sorry, dear, but I can tell you that it would be a long one. Jack's been a very busy man when it comes to plying his trade." She took a deep breath. "But then again, only the ones that know he was the one responsible should be looking for any kind of revenge. And you should be able to find those in the newspaper coverage of his career." Another laugh. "And if I know Jack, he probably has a scrapbook of them."

Hmm. A scrapbook of past crimes might turn out to be very helpful. If he would share it with us, of course. Given the nature of things, that wasn't a given.

"And the other thing that came to mind?"

"Well, there is the issue of the police just

showing up and basically going pretty much straight to the necklace in his pocket. I'm wondering if maybe, just maybe, one of them isn't a stellar officer." She glanced over at me. "The Oak Hill Police Department isn't like your Wind's Crossing Sheriff's Office. With a bigger town, well, sometimes people slip into the force that really don't belong there."

I stared at her. "You mean you think maybe the cop planted it there?"

She lifted a shoulder. "It's possible. That would explain a few things, wouldn't it? Like how whoever is behind this got into Jack's house to plant it? He might not have let Merlin and me set wards up for him, but he has a lot of really decent locks on his doors and windows. Breaking into his home wouldn't be something easy to do."

Another fine point.

After that, the conversation went in other ways, and we talked about life in general. It was a pleasant ride, even if I was a bit nervous about Lily meeting Liz. I was still torn as to whether or not I should tell her about our house's spirit resident. But if Arc hadn't mentioned it to Merlin, then I should probably keep my trap shut too.

Of course, as far as I know, Arc wasn't going to the house right now with Merlin in tow.

Chapter 13

As it turned out, all my worry about the whole Lily meeting Liz thing was for nothing. When we showed up to deliver and set up my bed, there was no sign of her. Not even after taking Lily on a quick tour of the house and barn.

"Wow. Merlin was right. You guys really got a steal on this place. It's just about perfect for all of you." Then she looked at me. "But at that price, I'd say there has to be something wrong with it. Please tell me you had it inspected before signing the contract. I'd hate to find out that the place was a ticking time bomb."

"Yup and the inspections all came back good. Plumbing, electrical, foundation, everything is fine." Now the hesitation was mine. If she noticed, she didn't mention in. But then we were in the library office at the time. I think maybe, like me, she was a little distracted by all those unread books just sitting there on the shelves. "It would appear that the furnishings of this room came with the house. If you see any books you'd like to borrow, just let me know."

She nodded distractedly and then finally gave herself a small shake. "I would definitely like some time in here once you get all moved in, if you'd be willing. Some of those books look quite old... and interesting."

Yeah, I'd noticed that too. Not the average library of a twenty-something. Who knew what might be sitting on those shelves waiting to be discovered? There could very well be some rare and valuable finds there. Wouldn't that make Kyle mad as heck?

That's when I realized that I probably should have asked Liz before offering to loan out her books. If she'd been able to protect them this far from her greedy brother, I'd hate to make her think she had to protect them from me too. I'd have to make sure she knew Lily was one of a few that I trusted to return them. Hopefully, that would be enough to keep her from going all ghostly on us.

We carried in the mattress and all the bed parts and managed to finagle them up the stairs. I was really glad we'd started with my bed. That way we were getting the hardest part over with first. Arc and Ruby had already stated they were going to use their upstairs loft as a recreation room. I imagined a big-screen television and theater seating was in the loft's near future.

Unfortunately, however, I had no idea which downstairs room they had chosen for their bedroom. The best we could do was park the bed parts inside the barn. They'd have to do the final move and set up themselves. Still, the biggest part would be done.

After that, the day went by quickly, and all with absolutely no sign of Liz. It was enough to have me a more than a little worried about her. Who knew one could worry about a ghost? I mean, what more could possibly happen to them, right?

Still, I know it made me jumpier than usual. Every little sound and I was looking over my shoulder, just sure that she'd be standing there. I had to find some way to get over that soon or living here would not be nearly as pleasant as I had thought it would be. And I'd had problems with Ruby's quiet shoes spell. That was nothing compared to living with a ghost.

Come to think of it, could I see her all the time? Or was it possible for her to fade in and out? Hmm. With the possibility of Opie moving in, or heck even just spending the night, that was a question I'd want answered sooner rather than later.

Once we had Ruby's bed delivered to their barn, Lily had left to do her own thing, and I started in again with the unpacking thing. First came my sheets. Once my bed was made, the place was really starting to feel a lot more home-like. It had me antsy to see the rest of my stuff here. Antsy to get my hands on more money to furnish the whole house, too.

All the furniture in my little three-room apartment wouldn't come close to filling this place up. We might have to branch out to other area bond agencies to get enough work to earn the money to do everything we needed to do. And get everything we wanted to buy.

But first things first. Jack.

I love libraries most of the time. If I'm looking for a book to read, generally fun-loving mystery novels, libraries are the place to be for me. Self-employed witches just don't have the budget to buy the number of books I go through every year.

But as much as I love libraries for their supply of reading material, I really disliked the little film reading area. It was clean to the eye, but something about sitting there and reading past issues of newspapers on that tiny microfilm just made things seem dark and dusty.

I couldn't let that stop me though. I had a free afternoon, and I needed furniture, dang it all. Plus, of course, I wanted to help Jack out. Part of me thought that maybe he should do a little more time in the pen as he obviously hadn't reformed his ways. But I could also see Merlin's point that he shouldn't have to do major prison time for a crime he didn't commit. The fact that he got by with many more jobs that he just didn't get caught on? Well, I was having a little trouble justifying all that. I could never be a criminal attorney, that's for sure.

By the time four o'clock rolled around, I'd gone through the past year and a half of local papers. And I had a shortlist of past victims of Jack Watson, burglar extraordinaire. When I say short, I meant it. I spent my entire afternoon just to get two names.

One of the cases, Merlin had got him off Scot free on a technicality. I could totally see that really ticking off the victim. To know that the police caught the man that stole their prized Poodle right before the big dog show and yet he got away with it? Yup, if someone had been counting on winning Best of Show in that competition, they would have been more than ticked off. They'd have been furious. The fact that they got their dog back the day after the show wasn't nearly enough to make them happy.

If anything, getting her back just seemed to tick them off even more. Maybe by then, they'd started counting the insurance money? Either way returning the dog was what ended up getting Jack caught to begin with. If he'd kept the darn thing, or handed it off to the one who paid him to do the job, he would never have been fingered for the crime to begin with.

Funny how that all worked out.

The other case had him doing time, but only a few weeks. More to the point, the woman got restitution for the value of her very unique and beautiful miniature bonsai garden, but the garden itself was never returned to her.

A few years back, I'd thought I wanted to grow a little bonsai tree. Right up until I did the research on them. They were a lot of work, and truthfully? The whole process seemed to be more than a little cruel to me. The end result was beautiful and stunning, yes, but countless hours and a lot of pain to the tree involved went into getting there.

Not something she could just go out and easily replace. I hope she got fair restitution at least.

And yes, by now, I wasn't such a stellar fan of Jack Watson. Both of these crimes seemed inordinately mean and petty to me. Funny how I could forgive someone for stealing jewelry and silverware. But dogs and trees? That was beyond wrong.

And something I fully intended to ask him about.

***

I was feeling pretty proud of myself by the time I got back home. It still sounded funny to call the new place that, but with my bed now fully in place, it was starting to seem more like it. Home. It sounded good.

I put my pack down on the floor by the front door and quickly climbed the steps. It might sound weird, but I really wanted to see my bed again. Small things can mean a lot sometimes.

The trouble was that when I finally reached my room—and my bed—it was to find my bed already occupied. By Liz. I didn't even know that ghosts could lie down. Go figure.

She must have heard me coming up the steps because she was facing the door with her eyes open and a big grin on her face.

"This bed is awesome! You'll be bringing your other stuff soon, too, won't you?" She really sounded hopeful.

"That is the plan," I said slowly. She had to know how the whole moving in thing worked, didn't she? Then, because I had to know, I asked. "Can you feel the bed?"

Her grin dimmed, and she shook her head. "No, but if I don't think about it too much, I can pretend it's just a really, really soft mattress. It kind of makes me feel alive again, having furniture in the house."

Her words hit me hard. It would be hard enough to be a ghost destined to haunt your old home for all eternity, but to have to do so in an empty and abandoned house was beyond cruel. I was beginning to not like her brother Kyle all that much. And I barely knew him.

"Well, there won't be all that much furniture even after I'm fully moved in, I'm afraid. I'm coming from a tiny little apartment and don't have all that much to move."

"That's okay. We all have to start somewhere."

That's true. And although I hadn't really planned on outfitting a guest bedroom, that was now totally on my to-do list. Only it wouldn't exactly be a guest room at all. It would be Liz's.

That raised a question, though. "Was this your bedroom?" If it was, I had a decision to make. I could keep it, or be super nice and change rooms. Not something I wanted to do as it would mean dismantling and reassembling my bed again. So, yeah, I was really hoping for a no.

It relieved me when she shook her head. "No, I used the room by my office." She shrugged. "I like being close to my books even while I'm sleeping."

That made sense. And made my new plan easier

to put into motion too.

"I'm glad you got to keep your desk and books, anyway. I'm guessing that couldn't have been easy."

She giggled. "It might not have been easy, but it sure as heck was fun. I had Kyle so freaked out, he ran whenever I came into the room. He might not have been able to see or hear me, but I made sure he knew exactly where I was."

My brain was working on the plan a little more. How cool would it be if I could buy her old stuff back? If she liked my bed, then chances were pretty good we had close to the same taste in things. If nothing else, just her bedroom furniture would be awesome.

"So, do you have any idea what Kyle did with your furniture and stuff?"

Her smile vanished, and her eyes narrowed. "Sold what he could for cold, hard cash. That didn't really bother me all that much. It was just what I expected him to do. But the stuff he couldn't sell? Like my files and paperwork and stuff? All that he took into the backyard and burnt in a big bonfire."

If ghosts could cry, right now she'd probably be bawling. Of course, I didn't have that limitation.

"He burnt your stuff? Really?"

Liz nodded. "Yes. And even that wouldn't have hurt so very badly—I mean, what am I going to do with it all now—but I'm fairly certain that my manuscripts were in that bonfire. I'd kind of hoped they'd be published after my death, but now the years I spent on them will just have been wasted effort." She wiped her eyes. Maybe ghosts could cry ghost tears after all. "And my agent was sure she'd be able to sell them too."

I looked at her in awe. "You're a writer?" Come on, that was beyond cool.

"You're using the present tense. I was a writer. Now I'm a ghost."

Maybe, maybe not. Yes, she was definitely a ghost. But did that necessarily mean that she was no longer a writer? Couldn't she tell her stories to someone and have them write them down? It wasn't like she'd lost the ability to think. It was kind of obvious that her brain still worked fine. Or whatever the ghostly equivalent was to a brain, anyway.

But then again, she would need a witch to be her transcriber. Better think that through before I shared that thought with her. How much time was I willing to devote to something like that? It wouldn't be so bad if I was a better typist. But there were reasons why office jobs just never really worked out for me. Typing was the biggest one.

As I said, I had some thinking to do. Right now, I kind of had my hands full as it was without adding anything new to the mix.

Liz's head tilted. "The others are home. Should we go and meet them?"

We did. I'd munched on a lunch meat sandwich and chips around noon, but my stomach growled like it hadn't eaten in days when I smelled the Chinese takeout in the bag Ruby was holding.

She gave me a look. "We'd have been here sooner, but Arc had to come and get me from the farmhouse. I'd kind of planned on riding over here with you. I don't have a car, you know."

And the pride I had felt about possibly making some headway in Jack's case just flew right out the window.

"I'm sorry, Ruby. I got tied up with some things. I found a couple of clues for Jack, though. And your bed is all ready to set up back in the barn. We would have done that for you, but I wasn't sure what room you wanted it in."

Her face wavered for a minute. I could tell that

she was trying to decide whether to hold on to her anger or go with the happiness of not having to spend another night on the leaky air mattress. That would be really important once she found out the familiars were rather demanding to be brought over to the house tonight.

Air mattresses and animals with claws really didn't get along all that well.

Finally, happy thoughts won out, and she gave me a smile. "All right, then, I'll forgive you this once. But from here out, you'd better be at the farmhouse and ready to give me a ride, okay?"

I hesitated. "This week, sure, I can do that. But we really need to think of a long-term solution. You might need to bite the bullet and get a car. Once we're fully moved in, I'll need to spend even more time on the bounty hunting thing if we want to make this work. Running out to the farmhouse every day will take time out of my day." Besides, once all my stuff was out, there wouldn't be anything there left for me, really.

Not counting the people, of course. It's not like I wouldn't still go and visit. Just not every single day.

"We'll work something out," Ruby said, waving off the issue. She knew I'd be on the hook until she got something else lined out. So did I.

"Now let's eat before the food gets cold. We still have a run to make tonight."

"We do?" Arc asked. "I'm kind of beat. Is it something you just can't live without until tomorrow?" He raised one eyebrow. "Or at the very least, something you girls could do without me?"

Ruby gave him a look, but I decided to play the nice sister. "Actually, Ruby and I can handle it no problem." I leaned into her. "It'll give us a chance to talk too." I had rather missed our solo one-on-one chats. Having a brother was nice. Having him around all the time, wasn't quite as nice.

She nodded. "I'll save my answer until I find out what the run is. If there's any lifting involved, Arc's coming along, whether he likes it or not."

"Nope, no lifting." I paused for dramatic effect. "The familiars have demanded to be brought over."

Ruby stared at me. "You mean your familiar, right?" Did she maybe look just a tiny bit green?

I grinned at her. "Nope, I mean our familiars, as in plural. It appears that Destiny has decided to become the spokes-cat for them."

Yup, she definitely looked a little green.

And it might have been totally self-centered and wrong of me, but suddenly I felt much better about being the one with the Goddess kitten.

Chapter 14

We spent that evening getting the familiars used to their new home. We took them on tours and walked the property line with them, so they knew where it was safe to go. That was important. Not that we thought they'd run off, but we needed them to know the boundaries. Now they did.

Liz finally showed up again about the time I was getting ready for bed. Arc and Ruby had gone back to their barn. No more communal camp out sleepovers, apparently. That was okay. I liked my space too. And it wasn't as if I was really alone, with Liz in the house.

"Where were you today, anyway? I was starting to get worried about you."

She tilted her head and just looked at me. "Why, what did you think could have happened to me?"

"Okay, I know it might seem a bit silly to worry about a ghost. But when friends disappear, you worry. It's only natural. The fact that you're a ghost hardly plays into that at all."

That got a smile. "So, we're really friends?"

"Yup. You're stuck with me now. When I make friends, it's generally a life-long thing." Then I thought about my words. "My life that is."

"Thanks." She hesitated for a few seconds. "Friends do favors for friends, right?"

Uh-oh, that didn't sound so good. But what kind of favor would a ghost want? If it was just to keep making Kyle's life miserable, I might be willing to take it on.

"Kind of depends on the favor, but, yeah, friends do favors for friends."

"Well, you asked where I was today. I was out in the woods out back. There's a little family of rabbits out there. It's funny, but when I was alive all I saw when I looked at them was food. Now, it's... different. They're really cute." She gave a fake shiver. Or maybe it wasn't so fake. Did ghosts feel the cold? "They're cold too. I think Winter is coming early this year, and I don't think they will make it without help."

"You were keeping them warm?"

She nodded. "Yeah, and I'll probably go back out for the night too. Unless..."

I was on board finally. "We could make them a little home?"

She grinned at me. "That's what I was thinking. It would be nice to have an actual pair of living hands to do things every now and again."

"Well, I'm not giving you permission to possess me, or anything like that," I said. I mean, friends or no, that would just be too creepy. "But if you tell me what you want me to do, I can be the hands for you."

A half an hour later, we took our home-made rabbit hut out into the woods. It was a simple little structure, and we'd had to improvise a bit on the materials to make it, as we didn't have any straw handy. Hopefully, it would do.

So, after a minor sacrifice of one medium-sized plastic tote and a couple of older sweatshirts, the little bunnies had a home. I wore gloves to keep my scent off the babies as I moved them in. The mother rabbit just watched us with wide eyes during the whole process. Well, at least she watched me. I wasn't at all sure that animals could see Liz. I'd have to remember to ask Destiny later.

"They can't."

Okay, maybe not so later then. I glanced over and saw my familiar sitting behind us, watching as the mother rabbit finally gave a little nod and hopped into the structure with her babies. I kind of understood now how the mother had stayed so calm through this.

"Thanks, Destiny."

She sniffed. "Nothing to thank me for. Just doing my part. This is a good thing you two did."

I nodded. It felt good, that was for sure. Then I turned to Liz. "When you were alive, you actually ate rabbits?"

She wouldn't meet my eyes.

"It wasn't all that unusual in my family. Just another meat for the table." She bent down and looked into the small opening we'd cut into the tote. "But they really are adorable, aren't they? I'm not sure how I missed that before."

"Well, if you're anything like me, you probably didn't want to think too hard about what your food was before it became… well, food. That would go double for me if the food happened to have been previously cute and fuzzy."

She nodded. "I guess that makes sense." She peeked into the tote one last time. "Goodnight bunnies. You're on your own now. This should keep you nice and warm."

We started walking back toward the house. Actually, I was walking, Liz was more like floating. She was going through the motions of walking though. It worked pretty well until you looked directly at her feet and realized they weren't really touching the ground. But who was I to question her right to hold on to whatever humanity she still could? Walk on, Liz. Walk on.

I had a little surprise for her when we got back to the house. She hadn't mentioned it yet, so I was betting she hadn't found it. I wasn't going to spoil it now.

We said goodnight, and I went into my room as she float-walked down the hall toward the office. It wouldn't be long now.

Sure enough, I heard her gasp of surprise. A few seconds later, she called out, "Thank you, Amie. This is awesome!"

Hey, it was just an air mattress all dressed up with sheets and a pillow, but after her remark about my bed, I'd thought maybe she would like it.

Looks like I'd guessed right.

Before I drifted off, I found myself wondering about Liz. Particularly the manner of her death and why she was a ghost. She'd said she might be in a kind of limbo as she'd never really gone out of her way to help anyone.

But today she had. Big time. She'd spent the whole day keeping those baby bunnies warm. Only a good person would have done that. It's possible that maybe she was improving her soul even after her death, but I really didn't think that was it.

I thought maybe Liz was a much better person than she gave herself credit for.

Which made me wonder what she was still doing here instead of being in her eternal resting place.

Something told me I needed to take a much closer look at her death.

Something told me that there was something very wrong there. And I'm a witch.

If witches know one thing is true in life, it's that our intuition is very rarely wrong.

***

The next day I spent digging in a little more into Jack's victims. At least the ones we knew about. It seemed to me that either of them would have a fine motive for setting him up. Personally, I couldn't blame them for that part of it. I'd be ticked off too.

But the fact remained that in order to set him up, they would have, themselves, had to commit the same type of crime that he had. That didn't feel right to me, but then again, the Mayor's wife wasn't a very popular person from what I'd been hearing. So maybe they didn't consider it a real crime.

Maybe they considered it more like killing two birds with one stone. Besides, according to their plan, the Mayor's wife got her jewelry back. So, technically, they only borrowed it.

My intuition was staying silent on this one. Darn it. I really wished it would kick into high gear soon.

In my digging, I found that the evening before the necklace was reported stolen, the Mayor had hosted a charity fundraiser right there in his own home. From what I was reading online about the event, pretty much the whole town had been invited. The guest list was an open call. That didn't really help to narrow anything down.

Too bad, too, as I was fairly certain that was the night the necklace was stolen. I checked the photos posted of the event, but she hadn't been wearing it that night. She'd went with pearls instead of her diamonds. Probably thought it made her look classier. There's just something about a woman in pearls.

But I did find one thing while I was going through the massive number of photos. I found Jack.

It was getting harder and harder to believe he didn't do it. And photo evidence of him at the scene of the crime really wasn't helping Merlin make any kind of case for his innocence either.

He really wasn't making this easy on us. At all.

Chapter 15

We'd all planned to meet up at Merlin's at six for dinner. According to Merlin, Lily would be joining the party and even cooking. My mouth was watering at the very thought of that. Pizza and Chinese food were good, don't get me wrong. I loved the heck out of them. But Lily's pot roast with carrots and potatoes? They can't hold a candle to that.

Of course, that might not be her menu for the night. That's okay too. I trusted a woman who knew her way that well around a kitchen.

This time I got to the shop early. They were staying open until five now most days. It would be a tight fit, but we should still make it to Merlin's in plenty of time. I knew what a stickler Lily was for punctuality. And she was not a woman you wanted to be on the wrong side of. There was something about her that I just couldn't put my finger on. Something kind of scary.

Lily was a woman who was far more than what she appeared to be. And I was definitely trusting my gut on this one.

I didn't get there early because I thought we'd run late, though. I got there early to visit with Opal and Kimberly. And yes, Nancy, Mason, and the baby too.

They had turned the back room into a nursery of sorts. And one of the rooms in the upstairs attic area, which had previously just been used as storage, had been changed into a playroom for the older kids. It worked. And, best of all, it allowed Kimberly to work and earn a wage. Not that she really needed it now that she was living at the farmhouse. But Opal liked us to all have our independence—and money too.

Kimberly was family now. I wasn't quite sure how or why that happened. But the night of All Hallows' Eve, something had changed the balance from a friend of the family to flat out family.

Luckily, all of us were okay with that. Also luckily, our little mini-estate had come along at the perfect time to open up the farmhouse for the newer arrivals. Kids take a lot of room. Even if they try hard not to.

After the shop closed, we headed for Merlin's at warp speed. Okay, maybe not that fast. But I wasn't exactly going speed limit either. I was pretty anxious about how the night would go. My mind, and my pack, were full of questions I wanted answers to. If I didn't get the answers I wanted, Merlin might not be a happy camper.

Because if I didn't get my answers, then Jack wasn't leveling with us.

And if Jack wasn't leveling with us, then I was turning his little British heiny in. Friend of Merlin's or no. I'd just have to find a way to do it and keep Merlin out of it.

There had to be a way.

***

With Lily's dinner cooking skills came Lily's rules. No talking business during dinner. We limited table talk to other, much more innocent things. Like how was your day, what I did last summer, and things like that.

And all the time I was biting my tongue wanting to get on with it already.

Finally, once the dessert was eaten—hot from the oven peach cobbler, Lily hadn't disappointed—and the table was cleared, we got down to it. I started things off by opening my pack and taking out my file folder. I'd come prepared.

The first item to go around the circle was a packet of pictures I'd printed off the Mayor's event website, clearly showing Jack. The last picture was particularly interesting to me. And the one I wanted a real answer to.

"If you'll all pay attention to that last photo, you'll see a man's bottom half going up the stairs in the background. That bottom half is dressed just like Jack is in the other pictures. I think you'll admit that he has a unique sense of style." That was actually putting it mildly. Someone should really tell the man that burglars should dress like everyone else to blend in. Not dress to stand out. But it had worked for me here.

"What I'd like to know is why Jack was climbing the stairs into the Mayor's private living quarters rather than staying below where the party was. I checked with some other people that went, and they said the upstairs was definitely off-limits. So, Jack?"

He hadn't even looked at the photos. He'd just let them pass by him in the circle.

"I don't think I like where you're going with this," he said. "I had thought we were all agreed that I'm a man of my word. I didn't take that necklace. You seem to be insinuating otherwise."

"And you seem to be evading the question," I said leaning in. "And I'd still like it answered. If I found this, then the cops found it. One more piece of evidence stacked against you. So, tell me, Jack, what is Merlin going to say about this when you're up on the stand in your trial? You can't hide out here forever, you know, and not being upfront with us isn't helping."

Jack shook his head. "I plead the fifth."

Merlin's eyebrow rose. Just the one. "I really don't think that's an option here, Jack. We've asked these three for help. Right now, it's starting to look like maybe you're playing us all for fools. I don't like that feeling."

Yeah, neither did I.

Now all eyes were on Jack. You'd think the man would look more nervous than he did. But no, cool as a cucumber my mom would have said. He looked cool and relaxed, but he wasn't saying anything, either.

"You know, if you truly didn't take the necklace, there is a very simple way to prove that to us," Ruby said thoughtfully.

I started smiling. I knew where she was going with this. Her truth spell. Just the thing for this occasion. But to abide by the council's rules, we had to have his permission before casting it on him. Then again, as he claimed not to believe in magic, that shouldn't be a problem, should it?

He glanced at her. "No need for any of your tricks, my dear. I'm willing to tell you why I was going to the upper level of the house, on one condition. That information stays between all of us. No matter what." He glanced over at Merlin. "Lawyer and client confidentiality extended to all of you if you get my meaning."

This was starting to get interesting. We agreed to

his terms, and he took a deep breath.

"I was on a job."

Merlin groaned. "Oh Lord, Jack, what have you done?"

It took me a minute, but I got there. "Let me get this straight. You did steal something that night. It just wasn't the necklace?" To me, that was a no-brainer. He was still guilty of the crime, in a way anyway, and to my mind Merlin should be okay with us handing him over.

That shouldn't break the agreement we just made at all. We'd agreed not to tell anyone what he said. We had in no way agreed not to act on it.

"But you told us you hadn't taken anything from that house." Merlin's face was a closed book. He was definitely not happy with how this was going.

Jack shook his head. "No. What I actually said was that I took nothing of value. I stand by that statement one hundred percent. That should be obvious as the item has yet to be missed."

"What did you take?" Merlin asked. "And if it wasn't of value, why take the risk?"

"Because it was a paid gig through the broker."

Ah, yes, that mysterious broker that no one knew who was. Or however one says that.

Arc looked thoughtful. Up to this point, he hadn't joined in. Now he did. "You know, I'm thinking it's high time we figure out exactly who this broker guy is. It's starting to sound to me like maybe he's the one setting Jack up. I mean, isn't it a little too coincidental? Jack being hired to do a job in the very house where the necklace was stolen. And then that stolen necklace being used to frame him? Awfully fishy to me."

Lily sputtered across the table. She'd been drinking while Arc was talking. She waved a hand and stood up. "Went... down... the... wrong pipe." She left the room, coughing and sputtering the whole way.

I started to stand, but Merlin waved me back down.

"I'll go check on her," he said. The weird part is that he didn't really look concerned. He looked more… well, puzzled than anything else. Like this wasn't at all the norm for Lily.

Or like maybe her reaction, and the drink going down wrong, had something to do with Arc's statement. But what?

She was friends with both men, surely she'd want us to sort this out as soon as possible. And Arc made sense. My new task would be trying to figure out exactly who this broker was.

Perhaps I was reading far more into this situation than what was truly there.

But my darn intuition was having a heyday.

There was time to nail that down later. Right now, there was work to be done.

We came up with a plan of sorts. One that would require more time in that dark corner of the library I disliked so much. Luckily, Ruby and Arc offered to handle that part of it.

My part was to keep checking out the victims. See if either of them had been at that party, or had other access to the Mayor's wife's jewelry. We did solve one part of the mystery though.

Jack had checked his coat at a fancy restaurant the night before the police searched his home. We were pretty sure that was when the necklace had been planted. It made sense. Especially with that particular hiding place. And all of Jack's expensive locks. Not to mention his newer security system.

According to him, he would think twice before trying to burgle a home so well protected. Which was kind of the point, wasn't it?

We were just starting to wrap things up, all of us

with our various tasks laid out ahead of us, when Mom and Archie showed up. Jack didn't waste any time hightailing it up the stairs. I really didn't think my father would be all that happy to know what Merlin was risking by harboring Jack.

Arc and Ruby gave hugs, and then they took off. Luckily, we had brought two cars to the meeting. I wanted a little Mom and Dad time.

Something I'd been sorely missing. I still missed having Mom in the same town as me. At least now, I lived a little closer.

"How is the moving in going, dear?" Mom asked.

I shrugged. "As well as can be expected. We won't get the rest of our furniture until Friday. That's when we've arranged to rent the truck. Even then, Arc and Ruby might be pretty set, I mean they have two apartments worth of furniture to fill their place with. I'll need to do some shopping as the funds come in."

"Actually, your mom and I have been talking about that," Archie said.

I held up my hand. "No. I don't want money from you guys. I need to do this on my own. Having my own place is the start of true independence, and that won't be worth all that much if I have to rely on money from my parents."

Mom laughed. "We know that, dear. We weren't going to offer you money." She gave Archie an I told you so kind of glance. It was pretty obvious that he'd suggested that very thing to her. "We were going to offer you access to the mansion's attic."

Huh?

Archie groaned. "I do wish you'd stop calling it that, dear. It's home. Not a castle. Not a mansion. Just… a nice home."

She reached over and patted his hand. "Of

course, you're right, dear." Then she looked at me. "We'd like to offer you access to our mansion home's attic. That place has been in Archie's family for generations, and over all that time, well, furniture has kind of built up. More than the house below could hold."

I stared at her. "Are you telling me that you have an entire attic of furniture ripe for the taking?"

She nodded. "Exactly. You'd actually be doing us a favor by clearing up some of the space up there. And some of the pieces are quite nice."

It still didn't seem right, taking it for nothing. Mom knew as well as I did that if they needed to clear the attic of nice furniture, all they had to do was call Opal. She'd take it for the shop in a heartbeat.

And they'd make bank on it too.

Mom knew me too well. "Yes, dear, we will be calling Opal in too. I'd love to clear it out soon. At least a room or two of it, anyway. But we want you to have first dibs. Anything that you see that you want is yours. Consider it a housewarming gift from your parents."

Archie smiled at me. "Moms and Dads are allowed to do this kind of thing, you know."

I swallowed. "That would actually be great." And it took a big worry off me too. It would be nice to mark a big expense off my list and still have my house furnished like an actual home.

We talked for a few more minutes, and then they stood to leave.

"It was quite a nice surprise to see you here, my dear," Archie said gathering me in for a quick hug. "If we had known, we wouldn't have made reservations for dinner. As it is, though, we need to head out if we're going to make it on time."

"You could join us, love," Mom said.

My stomach grumbled at the very thought. Not in a good way. "Sorry, Mom. Lily cooked tonight."

Mom laughed. "Enough said. We'll take a rain check then. Once you're all settled in."

Hugs went around the room, and they left.

I jumped when Jack spoke from directly behind me. How the heck was he so quiet?

"Merlin was telling me you three just bought a place together. Mind if I ask where?" Jack asked.

It might be wrong of me, but I hesitated a second before I told him. It wasn't like we had anything he'd be wanting to steal, right?

I was kind of surprised, though, when he got a thoughtful look on his face. "Are you talking about the big Cape Cod house with that massive barn out back?"

Now we were all looking at him. "You know it?"

He nodded slowly. "Oh, yes." He paused and looked over to Merlin and then back at me. "In the spirit of our new confidentiality agreement, I can say that I'm familiar with the place because I did a job there once a few years ago."

"You stole from Liz Jordan?"

Merlin looked at me. "You knew her?"

This time my hesitation was a lot longer. If it was common knowledge that witches could see ghosts, no one had ever passed that wisdom down to any of us. It wasn't something I really wanted to discuss in front of Jack. I'd for sure be telling Mom and Dad, no question there. But later. Like when I invited them over for dinner or something. I might even include Merlin and Lily too. Get all the family in on the secret. But Jack was no family of mine.

So I went with a vague, "Not in life, no." That pretty much covered it. Then I looked directly into Jack's eyes. "What did you take from her?"

He tilted his head. "Actually, I'm not quite sure. It was a blind gig. They told me to go in and retrieve a big cardboard box." He took a deep breath, then said with more than a touch of drama, "And I was specifically told not to look inside it."

"Did you?"

Jack looked affronted. "My dear woman, I may be a burglar, but burglars have work ethics too. They told me to not look. I took the job with its requirements."

In my mind, all his answer did was dance around the question. Something I found that Jack was very good at doing. If the answer was no, then a simple no would be much more convincing.

"And for the record, I didn't steal from Liz." He paused. "The timing was a tad odd, but the gig came through two days after she died. A sad thing that. I hate it when one so young is taken."

"Were there any markings on the box that might tell us what was inside it?"

"Sadly no. It was just an old paper box. Like the kind that holds several reams of paper that you buy from an office supply store. But whoever paid for the job knew exactly where to find it. They were very specific."

So what does one want so badly that they are willing to steal it from a dead woman?

Chapter 16

I had a very funny feeling that I knew exactly what was in that paper box. Liz's manuscripts. The weight of the box, according to Jack which was all we had to go on, would be about right for three completed books worth of printed out pages.

The problem was, I had mixed feelings about it. A small part of me was happy that at least the words that Liz had written might be seen by the world. They just might not have met a fiery death in the backyard after all. That was all good.

The bad was that it wasn't Liz that would get the credit for having written them. And that was very, very wrong.

I needed to get a copy of her original manuscript and go hunting for whoever had done this. All this kind of fit in with my theory that maybe Liz was still hanging around because her death hadn't been truly solved. The more I learned, the less I thought it was the accident everyone claimed it was.

But I needed that manuscript.

The next morning, I got the name of Liz's agent and went to pay her a visit. The address that Liz gave me wasn't in the best part of town. Not that it really mattered as the literary agency had moved offices. According to the nice people at the old place, they were now housed in the fancy new office building on Crane Avenue.

When I pulled up outside the building, I had to whistle. Liz's agent must do very well indeed to be able to afford office space here. There wasn't a free place to park, so I had to park almost a block away and hoof it back. Being early December in Michigan, it was cold. But at least it wasn't snowing, so I wasn't going to complain. At least not too much.

Just inside the building was a receptionist's desk. I made my way over to the nice-looking young man sitting behind it. He raised an eyebrow at me. Apparently, my jeans and leather jacket didn't exactly fill him with warm and fuzzy feelings about the nature of my visit.

"I'm here to see Alice Mayfield of the Mayfield Literary Agency. Could you please point me in the right direction?"

A touch of a knowing sneer crossed his lips, replaced almost instantly with a more professional look. "I see," he said. "You're a writer."

As if that would be a bad thing.

"Do you have an appointment?"

Okay, I was betting that Ms. Mayfield didn't hand over a list of all her appointments to this all-mighty front desk person. After all, he was the welcome committee for the whole building, not just her. I was also betting that if I said no to his question, I wouldn't be seeing Ms. Mayfield anytime soon. If at all, if he had his way.

He wasn't giving me much option here. So, I raised an eyebrow right back at him and stood a little straighter. "Would I be here if I didn't?"

He stared at me for a minute longer, then pointed toward the elevator. "The Mayfield Agency is on the second floor. Turn left, and it's the office at the end of the hall." Then his eyes went back to his computer, dismissing me entirely.

That was fine with me.

A short elevator ride and hallway walk later and I was opening the door to the agency. The agency's office suite had room for a receptionist of its own, but there wasn't one sitting at the rather small desk out front. The door to the inner office, however, was standing open.

"Hello?" I called out.

A tall and slender woman appeared in the office doorway. "Hello. May I help you?"

"I certainly hope so. Are you Alice Mayfield?"

"I am. Are you here seeking representation? Have you been published before?" There was a lot of hope in that last question.

"No, and no. Actually, I'm here about a former client of yours. Liz Jordan."

Her face lost a little of its color. "You are? I'm afraid there isn't much I can help you with. You do know that Liz died a few years ago, don't you?"

"Yes. A real tragedy that. And just when she had finished her great novel series too."

Alice swallowed. "Why exactly are you here?"

"If you don't have time right now, I'd understand, but I just wanted a few minutes to talk about Liz's books. According to Liz, you said they held real promise. That you were sure you could sell them. I'm trying to make that happen for her."

A little less color in her face now. She seemed frozen in place for a few seconds, then finally she backed back into her office and motioned for me to follow.

The outside office had been pretty bare, but this one was decked out to the hilt. Maybe she was just starting to get the agency going. This would be a pretty awe-inspiring office to meet with prospective clients. Obviously, the agency was having some success for its clients if it could pay for all of this.

She sat behind her desk, and I took the visitor's chair in front of it. Once we were settled, she cleared her throat.

"It had been my understanding that the manuscripts were lost around the time of Liz's death." She wasn't quite meeting my eyes, which had me a little worried. "I've been told that her brother destroyed all of her paperwork, including them, unfortunately, in a big farewell bonfire."

"Yes. I've been told the same thing. But you read them, so you had to have a copy, right? In this digital age, I'm guessing that meant that she emailed the files to you. So, you have an electronic copy of them, right?"

She hesitated, then shook her head. "I wish I did, but no."

"She didn't email them?" I was finding it really hard to believe that they had used paper files. That kind of thing just didn't happen anymore, did it?

"No, she emailed them. Unfortunately, that email account of ours was hacked and Liz's emails were destroyed. Unrecoverable, according to my IT guy."

"But if you were going to be shopping them to publishers, surely you had copies of the file from that email." I mean, something that important, there would have to be copies. You didn't just keep things like that in your email account. Only, from Alice's head shaking, I was guessing maybe she did.

The bonfire, the theft from Liz's house, now the email hacking, it was starting to appear as though the universe didn't want Liz's books to see the light of day.

Which, of course, only made me more determined to see that they did.

***

I had one more idea on how to possibly find a copy of Liz's missing manuscripts. Well, other than us finding the broker and tracking down the person who hired out the theft. That was still on the table too.

But right now, I just didn't have the time to follow up on that. I was due for a class on beginner Bonsai. It's kind of nice when things work out and you get to do interesting things while still working on a case. That was what this happened to be.

The teacher was Celeste Taggart, and she was Jack's victim number two. I arrived a few minutes before the class started and checked in my bag and jacket with the front desk of the small little school. Then I went around the room and studied all the pictures. It didn't take long to find what I was looking for. There had been pictures in the paper of the stolen garden. Pictures that pretty much matched the ones on the wall here.

Celeste saw me looking at them and walked over. "Gorgeous, aren't they? All the perfection of a forest in miniature."

"They're absolutely stunning." I wasn't just saying that either. Even the photos were taking my breath away. Imagine what the real-life garden would do? I liked Jack Watson less and less by the day. And regretted our decision to help him more too.

What did a nice guy like Merlin see in that guy?

I looked back at the photos. "I don't suppose it would be possible to see them in person? I know a picture is worth a thousand words, but the real thing must be worth a million. Or more."

She took a deep breath, and her eyes grew moist. "Oh, how I wish that were possible. But my tiny little piece of heaven on earth was stolen a while back. I'm afraid I'll never see it again. I just hope whoever has it knows how to take care of it properly."

"Someone stole it?" I'd been brushing up on my acting skills. I think I'm actually improving.

Celeste nodded. "Yes. And they caught him." She made a face. "I think he got like two weeks in jail or something, and they made him pay him the monetary value of the garden." A tear slid down her cheek. "As if you can put a price on a true Bonsai. They're more like children, we give so much of our lives to them."

And now I liked Jack even less. He'd stolen Celeste's baby, dang it. He should pay for that. And with a heck of a lot more than two weeks of jail time. If I had anything to say about it, he'd be making this right. Maybe he could steal it back?

"That's horrible!" At least now I didn't have to rely on my acting. I was speaking from the heart at this point. I leaned in a little closer. "If you know who took it, you could always try to get a little payment for it."

She just looked at me.

"I'm not talking about money. If the man took your garden child, I'd think you'd want a piece of his hide. I know I would."

All that got was a head shake. "That's just not the Zen way. If I let the anger fill me up to the point of retaliation, that only hurts me. Not him. That would be letting him steal far more from me than he already has."

The sad thing is, she really meant it. I could tell.

Celeste Taggart wasn't our framer.

That made me really happy. I liked her. I wanted the framer to be a bad guy, not an innocent and hurting victim of Jack's nefarious ways.

I still had one more victim to check out, but that would wait. I was going to learn about how to start a Bonsai.

Chapter 17

We'd decided on nightly meetings at Merlin's until we got this thing resolved. That made me happy. I had a few choice words for Jack, and I didn't want them bottled up inside of me for very long.

Tonight's meeting wasn't scheduled to start until eight to give Ruby and Arc time to hit the newspaper archive at the library after work. Of course, I was still Ruby's transport to get to Oak Hill. Her not having her own car and working several miles from home was getting old fast.

But as long as we were still moving boxes bit by bit, I really couldn't complain. I dropped by the farmhouse before picking her up and loaded up a few more boxes. I was surprised to find myself a bit teary-eyed by the time I was finished for the day.

By now, other than the large pieces of living room furniture and my table and chairs, my little apartment was pretty much bare to the bones. It felt…

sad. Like I was leaving a part of me behind.

I walked through the rooms, trailing my hand on the walls and remembering some of the best times I'd shared there. There were a lot. The farmhouse had been my home all my life. The only one I'd ever known.

Until now. It took a lot of getting used to.

Then I imagined the rooms as Nancy would decorate them in the years to come and smiled. She'd make it her own, for sure. Opal had told me that she'd already called dibs on my space.

Pretty cool to be eleven and already have your own apartment, huh? Of course, she'd really only get the back room all to herself for now. The other two rooms would be shared with Mason. Opal planned to take out the major appliances. The stove at the very least. The kids might get to keep the refrigerator if my aunt was in a giving mood.

The plan was to put Mason in my old bedroom next to the inside stairs—and directly across the hall from his mom—and then remodel the small kitchenette into a playroom for the older kids. What had been my living room would become Nancy's bedroom. And that would leave Ruby's apartment across the hall open for Kimberly and the baby.

Opal would have the whole downstairs all to herself. Well, except for having to share the larger kitchen when they planned full family-type meals together.

It was a good plan, and I was happy that things were working out. Kimberly needed the help right now, and Opal… well, Opal needed Kimberly and the kids. Yes, that had seemed odd to me at first, but that didn't make it any less true.

I loaded down the car and then drove into Wind's Crossing to pick up Ruby. I'd left enough room for her, but just barely.

She glanced into the car before squeezing into the small space remaining. "You remember we're getting a truck tomorrow, right?"

"Yes, and you remember that Mom and Archie have given us free access to anything we find in their attic that we want too, right? Unless I miss my guess, we'll be giving that truck a real run for its money tomorrow. You do still have the day off, don't you? And Arc?"

It made me feel a little guilty, but of the two of them, Arc was the most important for this endeavor. He was the muscles for the group. Come to think of it, I hadn't heard from my wonderful and loving boyfriend for two days. He was the other set of muscles. I'd better make sure to call him tonight and make sure he would be back for the big move in.

If not, Ruby and I would definitely have to man up. Not that we couldn't do it. We could. The two of us weren't exactly lightweights. But why would we, when we had big strong men willing to do it for us?

I dropped her off at the library and then went home to unload the car and do as much unpacking as I could without actual places to store stuff. Furniture comes in handy for things like that.

I'd only made it through two boxes, with Liz's curious eyes following everything I took out when the doorbell rang.

"Who could that be?"

Liz pulled a face. "Could be my worthless brother wanting his monthly payment a month early. It would be just like him."

I jogged down the stairs and glanced out one of the bigger windows that led out onto the main porch. I didn't like what I saw. Or should I say, who I saw?

According to the Goddess, who I trust implicitly, Patricia Bluespring and us Ravenswinds were all the same side now. But somehow, after all we'd been through with her, it still just didn't seem like it.

And now she was standing on my front porch. Taking a deep breath and forcing a smile on my face, I opened the door.

"Hello, Patricia. I take it your cell phone isn't working? I mean, if it was, you'd have called first, right?"

She glared at me. "Take a chill pill. I'm just here to drop this off." She handed me a thick file folder.

I took it, but didn't even open it. "What the heck is this?"

"It's your part of the job. You know, the one the Goddess gave us? Corruption in the council and all that? I split the council members between myself, you, Opal, and Ruby. I dropped off Ruby's share with Opal at the farmhouse."

She looked around her. "Imagine my surprise when Opal gave me your new address." She was talking in a very stilted voice like she was totally ticked off. Personally, I thought if either of us had a reason to be ticked off, it was me. She did show up unannounced. Nice people called first.

"Why? Did you think we'd live at the farmhouse for the rest of our lives?"

"No, but I sure as heck didn't think you'd be moving into Liz's old house. I tried to buy it myself, but the rat jerk Kyle wouldn't agree to sell it to me. He said that he'd heard witches could talk to ghosts. Have you ever heard anything so ridiculous? And his main fear was that Liz and I would talk about him behind his back. Like she's a ghost still hanging around this place." She grimaced and then glanced away. "And then he went and sold it to you, Ruby, and Arc. Three witches, just like me."

I hesitated. "So, I take it you knew Liz well?"

She nodded. "Being cousins helped that more than a little. But on her mother's side, thank the Goddess. I don't share any of the jerk's bloodline."

"I think maybe you need to come in." I stepped out of the doorway to let her pass the threshold, but she just shook her head.

"Thanks, but no thanks. I've done what I came to do, and now I'll get out of your hair."

"Um, Patricia, I really think you should come in for a bit."

"Why, so you can rub the fact that you have the house I thought I'd end up with in my face? Liz promised to leave this place to me, you know. But then, who expects to die in their twenties? No will, and the whole shebang goes to jerk-face Kyle."

"Yeah, she's really sorry about that."

Patricia's head whirled around, her eyes locking on mine. "What did you say?"

"She said I'm really sorry about that. I did mean for the house to go to you, Patty."

Now her head whirled around, taking her body with it, for the most part of the ride. Liz was standing right behind her.

I almost worried that she would get whiplash from all that head whirling, but as it turned out, whiplash would probably be the least of her problems.

When she woke up, that was. It might be a while. She hit the porch pretty hard when she fainted.

***

It was a good thing that Liz wasn't locked into just haunting the inside of the house. I'm not sure I'd have felt comfortable giving Patricia the run of my house. Even if all my stuff wasn't in there yet. As it was, they sat on the porch for their long conversation.

I felt bad about the chill in the air, so I took them out a blanket. Well, I took Patricia a blanket.

She looked at it in surprise. "Thank you, but I'm not cold."

Liz smiled up at me. "Temperature controlling ghost, remember? We'll be fine. You go to your meeting."

I hesitated, but in the end, I left them there chatting away.

When I got to Merlin's it was to find that Ruby and Arc were already there. I was the last to arrive. And in all the excitement I hadn't had a chance to eat, either. I was really hoping this wouldn't take long. Especially when I smelled the garlic on Ruby's breath. I'd be making a stop on the way home for sure. Italian sounded great right now.

I was really hoping to find Lily's van in the driveway and leftovers in the fridge, but that didn't happen. According to Merlin, Lily had other plans tonight and wouldn't be joining us. So, no home-cooked food for me.

Being hungry was just one more thing right now that increased my anger at Mr. Jack Watson. So, it really didn't surprise me when I was the first to lay into him. Again.

"How could you steal Celeste's baby? What kind of person are you?"

He looked at me, then Merlin, then back at me. "Excuse me?"

"The Bonsai Garden. How could you do such a thing? Do you know how long those things take to grow? The time it takes to nurture and care for them? It's like having a baby. And you stole it from her. Years of her life just poof. Gone in one little job of yours."

His cheeks colored. "Are they really that time-consuming? Like children?"

"They are. I spent a couple of hours this afternoon learning about them. They take a very special kind of person to create them. Which is obviously why the person hired you to steal it. They wanted the beauty but not the work. Only now, Celeste is worried that it won't survive the new owner. You didn't just steal her child, you filled her with worry for it. Forever."

He looked away. "I had no idea. I'm sorry."

"Are you really? Because if you are, then maybe you should start looking for a new line of work. One that doesn't exist to simply take away things that other people have worked hard for. Sometimes insurance money just can't replace what you've stolen, Jack Watson."

Now everyone was looking at me funny. What? They'd feel the same way if they'd seen Celeste's teardrop and her love for the craft of Bonsai.

I opened my mouth, more than likely to continue my tirade, but a ringing phone interrupted me. It was mine. Jack looked relieved.

Glancing at the number, it wasn't one I recognized. I swiped to dismiss the call and opened my mouth again, only to have my phone ring again. Same number. Whoever it was, they were persistent.

Then I remembered that Opie was still out of town. It could be him calling from a hotel or something. I answered it.

It wasn't Opie.

The voice was metallic sounding. Obviously doctored through some kind of device.

"I understand you've been looking for me. I think we need to talk."

Here we'd been looking for the broker, and they'd found us instead.

Chapter 18

At first, I was a little affronted when Arc held me back, and Ruby took my phone. Then I realized the double wisdom in their move. One, Ruby was our in-house negotiator. That was already an established fact.

Two, a hungry and ticked off Amie is probably not the person to handle a sensitive telephone conversation. I was most likely lucky they didn't break out the duct tape. Especially as Ruby immediately put the call on speakerphone,

I'd try to behave, but I wasn't going to promise that would be possible. I knew myself even better than they did.

"Are you the burglar's broker?" Ruby asked.

Metal Throat laughed. "I am. But I must say, I like that name. Burglar's Broker. I'm going to have to start using that."

"How did you know we were looking for you?"

See, right there Ruby proved her worth as a

highly-skilled negotiator. I'd have been yelling at her about the case in hand by now, while Ruby was asking very good, need to know kinds of questions.

"Ah, that's a secret of the trade, I'm afraid. And I think you'll find I'm very good at keeping secrets. I have to be."

I opened my mouth, and Ruby glared me to silence. I might be the Light Witch of the group, but Ruby's magic can be highly effective too. I knew better than to cross her. More importantly, she knew I knew that too.

"Well, if you intend to keep all your secrets intact, then why are you calling us?"

There was a brief silence. "I don't like the thought of my services being used to harm my worker bees. If that gets out, my little setup will fall apart rather quickly. Therefore, it's in my best interest to help you with this one."

Metal Throat had a point. I hadn't really thought about that side of things, but they were right. And I keep saying they when referencing the caller because, with the digitally enhanced voice, there was absolutely no way to know if the caller was male or female. Hence, they.

"Okay, then what are you willing to share with us?"

"I think it's important that you know that the buyer that hired out the gig to steal the necklace also hired out three other gigs. Four in total. That might sound like a lot, but most of my customers repeat far more than that. The ones who don't are generally one and done deals. Hiring four jobs is in between that and an anomaly all in itself."

"What jobs did they hire?"

"The first was the theft of a paper box from the home of the late Liz Jordan. As you might already be aware, Jack took that one."

Ruby glanced at Jack. "Do you know who this client is?"

"I do not. Extreme secrecy is part of my business model."

"And the other jobs?"

"The second was the theft of a computer from an office building. Both of those gigs were hired out a few years ago. Then nothing until just recently when the client hired two more in tandem. I thought it was rather odd as they specified Jack Watson as the thief for one of the jobs. Almost made me turn it down. But I gave that option to Jack instead."

I looked over at him. Jack shrugged. "What can I say? I have a reputation for being the best. It was rather nice being asked for personally."

"Only they asked for you personally to set you up," I said. Was the man really that vain? Apparently, the answer to that question was yes. Yes, he was. At least when it came to his work.

"And the other job I take it was the theft of the necklace?"

"Yes. I tried to tell them it would be far cheaper to have Jack nick it too as he'd already be there, but they were adamant about the gigs being by different workers."

I loved how Metal Throat called them workers. Like they were all part of a respectable business or something. I'd stayed silent long enough.

"I'm not sure I understand," I said. "If your client's sole intention was to frame Jack Watson for the theft of the necklace, why not have him actually steal it?"

"Probably because they knew I have ways to hide it that the police would never find. Not even if they searched my entire house. They've searched before with stolen goods sitting just inches from them, and they never found a thing." He straightened a little. "Putting a stolen piece of jewelry in my jacket pocket and then leaving it there for them to find? Wouldn't happen."

Okay, so that made sense. But hiring out all these gigs, as they called them, couldn't have been cheap. So whoever we were looking for must have money to spare. Or at least they did at the time.

"Can you give us the name of the office building the computer was stolen from?"

"Certainly. It was taken from the office of Tatum and Howard Architectural Engineering. "

Never heard of them, but then I'd never heard of any of this a week ago, so what did I know?

"And now, dears, I'm afraid you know everything I'm willing to tell you. Finding me at this point would do you no good. We are done."

"Don't hang up!" I said. "If you've told us all you're going to, then I have something to tell you, and maybe ask you too."

"Go on."

"I want you to know that I think you did a despicable thing arranging for the theft of that Bonsai Garden." I might be harping a bit too much about it, but meeting Celeste and learning a bit about the craft really had my motor running on this one. What they had done went far beyond simple burglary. It came very close to kidnapping.

And I basically repeated my earlier tirade to Jack to Metal Throat. In the end, there was silence.

Finally, they spoke. "You make a very valid point, dear." What was it with this person calling us all dear? "Perhaps I should try to vet my clients a little more thoroughly in the future. Whether or not you choose to believe this, I'm not a bad person. I don't like the thought of my workers taking things that will actually cause serious hurt to people."

"I think that might be a very good start, anyway." An even better one would be to give up the business altogether, but I could tell by now that would not happen. Not anytime soon.

"And the thing you wanted to ask?"

"I know you won't tell us who the buyer of the garden or any of the other jobs are, but is there any way to find out? I'm thinking if I can get together the money, I'd like to arrange a theft of my own."

Another laugh. "Well, isn't that an interesting turn of events? I'm taking it perhaps you want the Garden yourself?" Then they hesitated. "No, that wouldn't be you at all, would it? You want to return it to its rightful owner, don't you? And you're willing to pay for that?"

"As I said, I'll have to get the money together, but yes, I'm willing."

"Fine. I'll text you an email address. Use it when you have the money. Jack can give you my standard fee. In the meantime, I'll see what I can pull together to identify that client. Then I'll be smashing this phone. Tracing it back to me isn't on the table."

And they were gone.

The others were just staring at me. "What?"

Arc came over and put his arm around me, effectively capturing both my arms to my side at the same time. "Think about it for a minute, Amie. If the broker was willing to research the identity of a gig buyer, wouldn't it make more sense to have them working on the buyer of the necklace gig?"

Crapsnackles.

***

Opie called while I was stuffing my face with a huge double-decker hamburger and fries.

"Isn't it a little late to be binge eating?" he asked.

"Ha, when it is ever too late to eat?" After all, that was one of the things we had in common. Our great love of food.

"True, true. Hey, Amie, love of my life? How mad are you going to be when I tell you I'm going to miss moving in day?"

I finished chewing and even swallowed before answering. "Well, since I'm guessing it involves you spending more time with Missy rather than helping your girlfriend move heavy furniture into a new house, what do you think?"

"Hmm, that mad, huh? I was afraid of that. But, um, something's come up here, and I can't leave Dad right now."

Okay, I was starting to get worried. I really cared for the sheriff. If he was in trouble, then bugger the move-in day.

"Where are you? Do I need to come? Scratch that, I'm coming. Just tell me where."

"I actually can't tell you that, and please do me a favor and don't try to have Tommy track my phone for you, okay? Me and Dad are perfectly fine. We just got into a kind of tricky situation that requires we stick around here for a few more days. I'll tell you all about it when I get home."

I could tell he was holding his breath for my reply, even over the phone. It was something he did.

It took a minute for me to consider my options. Yes, I could contact Tommy and yes, he could probably track them down by the cell phone coordinates or something far above my mental capacity with technology. But did I really want to do that? Isn't part of being boyfriend and girlfriend trusting the other party enough to believe them when they say they're fine?

Actually, if he'd said they were fine, I'd have been more likely to believe him. The perfectly fine was stretching it. Something was up. Besides, he seemed to forget who he was dealing with here. If I really wanted to find him, I could just cast a find spell. No Hot Geek required for that.

I glanced at my watch. It was almost ten o'clock. We were getting the truck in a little less than twelve hours. I needed some sleep.

"Amie?"

My hesitation must have lasted longer than his capacity for holding his breath.

"All right. I'll give you another twenty-four hours." He started to say something, but I cut him off. "Call me at ten o'clock tomorrow night, and we'll talk about an extension. I'll expect more details then, got it?"

A breath blew into the phone. "That's the best deal I'm going to get, isn't it?"

"You got that right."

"Okay then, I'll talk to you in twenty-four hours."

"One more thing, Opie."

"Yes, Amie?"

"If my phone hasn't rung before five minutes past ten tomorrow night, I'm casting a find spell and coming to get you. Understand?"

"Yeah, I kind of forgot about that for a minute. I'll call." He hesitated. "I love you, Amie. Thanks for trusting me on this. It means a lot."

"Yes, well, don't make me regret it, okay?"

"Deal."

"And by the way, I love you too, you dork."

"I know." And he hung up. I'll never get how guys can do that. Just end calls in a split second.

I pushed the disconnect on my end, not that it really mattered, and finished my food. I was still sitting in the parking lot of the restaurant. It might mark me as odd, but when dealing with a fast food meal alone, I'd rather get the food from the drive-through and then sit in my car and eat. Going in just took too much effort.

And as hungry as I was when I got there, no way was I waiting to eat until I got home.

I was just finishing the last bite when my phone rang again. This time it was Ruby.

"Hey, Amie, just wanted to call and say how nice it was of you to give me and Arc a head's up about the whole Patricia Bluespring situation. Arc was thrilled when we came home to find her here."

Double crapsnackles.

"Sorry about that. Metal Throat kind of threw me off my game."

"Who?"

"Metal Throat. You know, the broker."

She giggled. "Okay, you mean kind of like Deep Throat, right?"

Well, duh. "Besides, I really would have thought she'd be gone by now. That was hours ago."

"Yes, well, apparently she and Liz have a lot of catching up to do. Liz wants to know if you have a problem with Patricia spending the night. She says she can sleep on the mattress you gave her in the office."

I hesitated.

Ruby's voice lowered. "You know you can't really say no, right?"

Yeah, I knew that. "Okay. Tell her it's okay with me, then." Even if that wasn't actually the case.

Chapter 19

We should have gotten a bigger truck. A much, much bigger truck.

Archie, AKA Dad although it was still hard for me to call him that, had a huge attic space. And Mom had been absolutely right when she'd said it was crammed to the gills with furniture. There was furniture up there that spanned multiple generations. Some of it had to be far older than the house itself. And that was saying something.

Opal's eyes widened when she saw it. I could see the mental wheels spinning at the thought of how much she could make off all this. But it surprised me when she told Mom that it wouldn't be smart to sell it all off. Some, yes, enough to make room, but according to Opal some of this furniture was the stuff that dreams were made of and would only increase in value as time went on.

Of course, the first surprise Opal had given me

that day was leaving her precious shop in the hands of a non-family member. I hoped that Kimberly realized just what a milestone that was for her. It was rather a singular occasion. To me, that meant that Kimberly and her small brood were permanent members of the Ravenswind family.

We ended up taking three truckloads of furniture off their hands, and I swear we didn't even put a dent in the attic space. I took a beautiful living room set, complete with a sofa, a loveseat, two chairs, and a matching coffee table and end tables. Then I got a cute full-sized bed frame with a built-in bookcase and matching dresser to deck out a guest bedroom—I was really hoping that Liz would like them, as I planned to put them in her old bedroom. Just for her. I also got a full dining room set complete with a hutch.

I could have taken more with all the rooms in my new home, but with the furniture I had already, it was enough for now. And it would still be here later if I decided I wanted more. It wouldn't be right for me to take all the truck space just for myself.

Like Ruby would let that happen. She and Opal went through the pieces with wide eyes and picked out a full household of furniture that would go perfectly in their rustic barn. Several generations of furniture meant that there was truly something for everyone up there.

Once we got all that moved in, we still had our respective apartments to clean out. Even with the early start, we were still working hard moving things in when my phone went off at ten o'clock precisely.

"Hey, Opie. Is it too late for me to change my mind about being okay with you not being here? You're really missing a lot of fun. And by fun, I mean back-breaking hard work."

"I'm really sorry, Amie. You have no idea just how much I'd rather be there with you right now. Hard work or no."

He sounded tired. And stressed. Very, very stressed.

I took the phone out onto the porch. It was chilly, but there was too much noise inside for this type of conversation.

"I think it's time you told me what's going on, and just how Missy's involved in it."

"Well, yes, Missy's involved, but not how you might think. She's gone missing. Van is a wreck. It was like she was there one minute and gone the next. He's kind of freaking out. He's called in his dad to help."

I felt my eyebrows shoot up.

"And yes, Van's dad is still very much alive and kicking. He's a very... unique... individual. Did you know that Van and his family are elemental witches too? Like you guys? Came as quite a shock to Dad and me."

Yeah, I knew all right, but as it had been told to me in confidence from Giovanni himself, it hadn't been something I could actually share.

If Giovanni had pulled his dad into it, what did that mean? "Is Van thinking her disappearance has something to do with magic?"

"At this point, we just don't know. But Dad's made arrangements for the two of us to stay on here until we find her. I really hope you're okay with that. For what it's worth, we aren't doing this as much for Missy—although I'd be lying if I said it wasn't partially that—as we're doing it for Giovanni. He has Dad really worried right now."

I was wavering. I glanced behind me at the house that desperately needed organizing and setting up. I was torn. I liked Giovanni, and I didn't like the idea of him suffering.

"Did she go missing before or after the wedding?"

"Just after the I do's, actually." There was the sound of voices in the background, and I could tell that Opie held his hand over the mic on the phone to answer them. "I've got to go, Amie. Same time tomorrow?"

I swallowed. "Okay. But if you need me, you know all it takes is saying the word, right?"

"We know that, but thanks for saying it anyway. Van's dad is pretty powerful. I know you're a Light Witch and all, but from what I've seen, he might be able to give you a run for your money. The man is nothing but raw power."

"Why do I feel like there's a 'but' in there somewhere?"

"Probably because I haven't told you how much you and Rosati senior have in common. He doesn't much care for Missy either."

Hmm. Sounded like a man I could grow to like.

"Love you." And he was gone before I could tell him I loved him too. So I texted it. We witches believe in Karma, and it seemed like the thing to do. Besides, that way he had it in writing.

***

We got everything pretty much in place before calling it quits for the day around midnight. The next morning, I looked around at all the unopened boxes I could now unpack and put away, and I was kind of, sort of over the whole moving thing.

Having a new home was awesome and exciting, yes, but after almost a full week of doing the moving in process, I was more than ready for a break. Besides, to be honest, having Patricia Bluespring in my home was freaking me out more than a little.

At least she had taken off that stupid council hat. That had made her seem a little more approachable anyway. And trust me, with Patricia, every tiny bit helped immensely.

I heard voices downstairs and then the heavenly smell of bacon frying drifted up the stairs. I followed my nose.

"I hope you don't mind me making myself at home in your kitchen," Patty said, after giving me a short nod. "But I made enough for two. And Liz won't be eating, so that means plenty for you."

A glance at the table showed two plates full of bacon and eggs. There was even a plate in the center with pancakes and a small pot of warmed maple syrup beside it. I took a deep breath, gathering in the wonderful scents of a homemade breakfast.

Maybe having Patricia here wasn't so terrible after all. Not that I'd want to make it permanent. I had already chosen my housemate, thank you very much. I'd even left a couple of rooms empty for his stuff too. I didn't want to do the whole house without him. I wanted him to be a part of it.

We sat down to eat, and Patricia looked over the table at me. "I'm still pissed about Kyle not selling me this place, you know." Then she made a face. "But I can't really blame you for taking advantage of his desperation to sell it, either."

She paused, and my instinct kicked in. So I tried to beat her to the punch. "I'm really sorry Kyle was such a jerk to you about it, Patty." Her eyebrows rose at the shortening of her name, but I kind of liked it. It brought her down a little more to my level. And after all, she called me Amie, not Amethyst. Fair is fair. "But the truth is, I'm not interested in selling. We've gone through a lot already to make this happen for us, and I don't see the others feeling any differently than I do about that."

Patty took a deep breath and nodded. "I was

afraid of that." She took another bite and chewed thoughtfully. "I don't suppose you'd be willing to let me visit on a regular basis? I promise to keep my hands off any of your stuff, and I give Liz full permission to tell you if I break my word on that."

I had to think about it. "Define a regular basis. Are we talking monthly, weekly, or daily? It makes a big difference you know."

"Well, for starters, I'd like to make it a couple of times a week at the very least. Liz and I have a lot of catching up to do. We didn't visit as much as we should have in the last few years of her life. So there is a lot of ground to cover." She glanced at Liz and then back to me. "And I know Liz doesn't want to hear this, but I'm not at all convinced that her death was accidental. If I'm right, I want to find the person or persons responsible and make them pay."

What do you know? The two of us had something in common after all.

"I agree with you. I have my doubts, too, especially with some new developments that have cropped up in the last few days. But I hope by making them pay, you are talking about turning them over to the authorities. Not doing some kind of hex."

I was all too familiar with Patty's hexes. They were pretty potent things.

"They would earn a lot more than a smelly car; I can tell you that much." She took another bite. "But the two aren't mutually exclusive, you know. I could turn them over and hex them too." She looked thoughtful. "Yes. That sounds about right actually."

"I think the two of you will be disappointed when you find out I was just clumsy, had a dizzy spell, and fell down the stairs all on my own," Liz said. I noticed that she'd been watching us eat with interest. It was making me feel guilty.

Then Patty's eyes snapped to mine. "Wait a minute. What new developments?"

And then I was in a conundrum of my very own making. How much could I tell Patty without admitting that we were helping a known criminal evade the law? Being on the council, Patty was an adamant believer in abiding by the rules. Even the ones that didn't particularly make sense. Or were just plain wrong.

It was one of the main reasons she still had no idea I was a Light Witch. I wanted to keep it that way, too.

"I've been working on another case, and as these things sometimes happen..." I glanced at the ceiling to show that I was talking about the higher power here. From the look on her face, I think she got that pretty darn quick. "It would appear that the case I'm on is tied somehow to Liz. Or, more specifically, to Liz's missing manuscripts."

"Missing? But I told you that Kyle burned them," Liz said, shaking her head. "They aren't missing. They're gone."

"Maybe not." I snagged another bite and chewed slowly, drawing it out. "I have it from a fairly trustworthy source that a paper box was stolen from this house just after you died, Liz. Before Kyle had a chance to go all Pyro on your stuff."

Liz's eyes actually glowed. Okay, so that was weird. She leaned toward me. "An office store paper box? From beside my desk in the office?"

I nodded. That's where Jack had said it was all right.

She bounced, or rather floated, up and down on the chair. Who knew ghosts could get so excited about worldly things?

"Then that means my words are still alive! Oh, this is so awesome." Her glowing eyes met mine. "Do you think they'll publish them? Oh, that would be so wonderful! To have people actually reading my books." She jumped off her chair and ran over to me, throwing her ghostly arms around me.

It gave me goosebumps. Getting a ghost hug was a very singular experience.

"You do know that if they have them published, it's very likely that your name won't be anywhere on them?" Patricia said softly, not wanting to dash her feelings completely.

Liz nodded. "That's okay. People will be reading them. That's really all that matters to me. I'd have been using a pen name anyway, so I never meant my name to be on them when they published." She danced around the room. Literally danced.

"But they stole from you," Patricia said, with a glance over at me. "They shouldn't get away with that."

Liz stopped and turned to face her cousin. "Think about it. If Kyle had known what they were and published them, he'd have profited from them. That wouldn't be nearly as much fun as watching them go out into the world and knowing that he'll never see a penny from them."

Patty's eyes widened. Maybe she had never realized just how much Liz disliked her half-brother. It was starting to really make me appreciate mine more. I must have won the half-brother lottery with Arc.

"Well, I see why you might be happy about that," I said around a bite of pancake. "But I'm afraid I have to side with Patty on this one. Thieves shouldn't get away with their crimes. They should pay."

Patty looked at me from across the table. There was a lot in that glance we shared that we didn't want to say out loud in front of Liz.

Because the possibility was that whoever had paid to have the manuscripts stolen also had Liz killed.

Whether they did it themselves or had it done, Liz's books just might have gotten her killed.
And that simply couldn't stand.

Chapter 20

I had a bad feeling about that other gig that
Metal Throat had told us about. The stolen computer
from that office building. But still, I wouldn't know until
I checked it out. I felt like I owed it to Liz to cross all the
T's on this one. I wanted to find those manuscripts. I
hoped that once I did, it would lead me to the one who
had taken them.

And justice could then be served. We'd worry
about the whole Kyle profiting from it angle later. There
had to be a way to keep him out of it. We were smart
people. We'd figure something out.

So once Patty left for work, I got ready for a
visit to Kyle. Something was telling me I really needed
to get to know him a little better. Find out why the two
partial siblings felt so strongly against each other. There
was something there.

Destiny was still lounging on my bed when I
went in to change. She opened her little kitty eyes and
stared at me.

"Don't worry, I saved some bacon for you." I

placed the small little saucer over next to her water dish and went into my closet, past a ton of taped-up boxes, to pull out a fresh pair of jeans and one of my dressier sweatshirts.

"I don't suppose you have any words of wisdom for me today?"

She blinked up at me. Then she stretched and yawned. Only after going through the whole kitty cat waking up routine did she bother to answer me.

"What did you have planned today?" She looked around at the heaps of cardboard surrounding the bed and other furniture. I got the message.

"Yes, I know I need to finish unpacking, but today I plan to visit Liz's brother and see if I can't track down her old computer. I'm hoping that if I can get my hands on it, I can have Tommy work his magic and retrieve the manuscript files even if Kyle has already deleted them. I've heard stories that can be done."

Destiny tilted her head at me. "And that will accomplish what exactly? You heard Liz; she is perfectly happy just to know that her words live on. You seem to be taking this far worse than she is."

I considered that for a minute. She wasn't wrong. In the end, I gave a small shrug. "That might be true, but it's something that bothers me, and I want to get to the bottom of it all. Besides, there is still the possibility that Liz's death wasn't the accident everyone thinks it was. And I'd be checking up on it anyway as it was one of the gigs that Jack's framer bought."

"Who are you talking to? And who is Jack?"

I looked up to find Liz standing in the doorway.

"I'm talking to Destiny. She's more than your average cat."

Liz came over and looked down at her. "Really? She looks pretty average to me."

Destiny hissed, and I had to turn away to hide

my smile. I bet pretty average was never something the Goddess had heard in relation to her looks before.

"Trust me, she's not. And Jack is the case I'm working on." She opened her mouth, and I held up a hand to stop her. "No, I'm not going to tell you about it. Not yet. I'm sorry but I just don't know you all that well yet." Plus, there was the whole Patricia Bluespring thing.

She looked disappointed, but she gave a nod. "I understand." She paused, moving her finger above the design of my bed's comforter. "I got the impression that you didn't like my cousin much. She said you two kind of had a history."

I laughed. "That's putting it mildly. She tried to put Arc in a witches' prison."

"Arc? Really? Why?"

"Well, to give the devil her due, at the time it did rather look like he'd killed his girlfriend. But the real reason she was out to get him was an old grudge against his father. We've got all that straightened out though. We're cool now."

She just looked at me and raised one eyebrow. "Really? I must be reading you totally wrong then, because I don't think you like her any better now than you did then."

Well, a little better maybe. But there was always that possibility of her finding out exactly what I was and putting me into a magic draining box for the rest of my life. Kind of hard to get past that to actually start liking someone.

When you liked someone, you generally started trusting them. And that led to dropping your guard around them. Something I couldn't afford to do around Patricia Bluespring.

I liked my life the way it was, thank you.

But how do you explain all that to someone you couldn't afford to explain it all too? You didn't.

So I just went with a shrug. "Gaining my trust is a long process. Just the way I'm built, I guess."

"I get that. I was way harder to get to know back when I was still breathing. Having three years with no communication between me and another soul, living or dead, kind of changed that."

I smiled at her. "You're doing well if you ask me." I glanced down at the clothes. I could ask her to leave so I could dress, but why? It wasn't like I was shy. Witches are pretty used to nudity.

I shucked off my clothes and started dressing. It didn't seem to bother her. But then, I have no way of knowing if she had seen me naked before or not. It appeared she had the ability to appear and disappear at will. Kind of threw privacy out the window, that.

"Any tips on how to handle your brother?"

"You're really going to see him? Of your own free will? Why?"

Funny, she was getting really good at asking questions, but not so good at answering them.

"You wrote on a computer, right?" She nodded. "Well, I'm trying to track it down. I'm guessing Kyle wouldn't have thrown that into the fire."

She laughed. "You're right there. Anything he thought he could sell or make a quick buck off of, he took. But the papers, and my life's work? That was totally worthless to him."

"Is there a reason you two didn't get along? I'm sensing there is."

"His mom left them when he was a teenager. A year later, Dad married my mom and then I came along. I think Kyle thought if the two of us weren't there, maybe his mom would come back. He kind of made our lives miserable. Mine especially. Mom and Dad weren't always around." She gave a small shiver.

"I'm sorry. Maybe we can work out a fitting hex

to put on him if you'd like. Or at the very least a Karma spell. If he's as bad as you say, that would work well, and there's less backlash from that kind of spell because we let the universe decide his fate."

She giggled. "I know Patty's a witch, but I never really understood how all that stuff worked. Do spells really work?"

I grinned at her. "They do. But don't feel bad about not believing in witches' power. Until I met you, I didn't believe in ghosts either."

Liz got quiet for a minute. "About Kyle… don't go sneaking around his place at night, okay? It wouldn't be safe. He's ex-military, and he keeps a lot of guns at the ready. He's definitely a shoot first, ask questions later kind of guy. I don't want you getting hurt."

"Thanks. But all I plan to do is talk to him. In broad daylight. No guns involved." Although her words reminded me to dig out my taser and throw it in my bag. One could never be too careful in this crazy world of ours, and I'd grown lax in carrying it. Now that I was working again, that needed to change.

I took Liz's words more to heart than you might think. When dealing with people like her brother Kyle and his stockpile of guns, it was good to be careful and on your toes at all times. Crazy didn't only come out at night.

He lived in a modest little house in a good neighborhood in Oak Hill. The house wasn't at all what I expected. It looked like a nice small family home. The home of a sane person. I was having serious doubts that sane didn't exactly describe Kyle Jordan.

Even if he was sane, he most definitely wasn't nice. Who took their problems out on a baby and child? I thought of Nancy and all the trouble she had growing up without a mother. It sure as heck hadn't turned her into a bully. Quite the opposite.

After parking at the curb, I took a deep breath, opened my car door, and stepped out to face Kyle's front door. There was a very prominent No Soliciting sign hanging to the right of it. To the left was a sign warning that he didn't dial 9-1-1 with the picture of a rather large pistol.

Yeah, Liz had been right about not snooping around here after dark.

Another breath or two, and I stepped up the one small step and onto his tiny little porch. The door opened before I even had the chance to knock.

Kyle stood before me. His eyes were a little wild. "I don't care what you have to say. You had inspections done. If they didn't find anything structurally wrong with the house, and they didn't, you don't have a leg to stand on. You three signed the papers, and it's a done deal. No backsies."

I stared at him for a minute. This was one of those days where it didn't take much to confuse me, it would seem. Then I shook my head at him.

"I'm not here about that. I just want to talk with you if you have a minute."

He didn't look like he believed me. "You aren't going to try to back out of the deal?"

"Nope. We kind of like the place."

His eyebrows rose, but after a brief hesitation, he stepped back and let me in. "What is it you want to talk about?"

I took a quick glance around the place before I answered. Kyle should really spend some of the money from our little deal and get himself a house cleaner. Sooner rather than later too.

He saw my glance and grimaced. "I've been sick. That's why the place is such a mess. It isn't usually like this. You just came over at a bad time."

Yeah, sure, Kyle.

"Look, if you've been sick then you probably aren't up to a long visit, so I'll get right down to it. I'd like to buy Liz's computer."

His eyes widened when I mentioned Liz's name. "You knew Liz? You all didn't tell me that."

"No, we didn't know her. But I do know that she was writing novels, and I'd really like to get my hands on those manuscripts. I'm guessing that there might be a copy of them on her computer. Do you still have it? I'm willing to pay good money for it."

"If you didn't know her, then how do you know she was a writer? I got rid of all her paperwork." His eyes widened even further, almost to the point of popping out of his skull. At least it sure looked that way. "Crap. You aren't a witch, are you?"

What does a witch say to that? Deny my Goddess and say no? I don't think so.

"I am. But what does that have to do with me buying Liz's computer?"

"You've seen her then, haven't you? Liz. I know she's there, so don't even try to lie to me about it."

I didn't like the look he was giving his desk drawer. It looked to me like he was starting to panic, though I had absolutely no idea why. But I guessed that drawer held a gun of some type. Not that he'd ever make it to it without me hitting him with my taser.

I blew out a breath. "Okay, so you got me. I've seen her."

"Dammit. I never would have sold that place to you if I'd known you were a witch." Another glance at the drawer. Then he looked back at me. "But you don't wear that stupid pointed hat like most witches."

Well, no, mostly only council members wore those. And only those that were more interested in status among the witch population than actual fashion sense. Ones like Patricia.

"I really don't know what your problem is, dude. Yes, we've seen her, but she's friendly. It isn't a deal-breaker on our end, so why should you have issues with it?"

He stared at me for a minute. "Because I know you witches. You use Ouija Boards and seances to speak with the dead. Liz hated me. Anything she says about me is an outright lie. Now I think you need to leave."

"Not until you answer me about the computer. Do you still have it?" I gave a pointed glance around me. "Cold hard cash would allow you to hire someone to help you clean this place up."

That got a glare. "As a matter of fact, I don't have it." He opened the front door and took my elbow. "It was stolen from my office before I… quit."

And with that, he pulled me the few feet back out onto the porch, not that I resisted going, and shut the door in my face.

Our little talk was done. But what an interesting talk it had been.

Kyle was afraid of something that Liz might tell us. But what? That he was a bad person? Shoot, we already knew that. Who sells a haunted house without warning the buyers?

And who takes their troubles out on an innocent little half-sister?

But he had confirmed what I came to find out. The computer that the theft buyer—what does one call them?—had stolen was indeed Liz's.

The same buyer had ordered the theft of the manuscripts, the computer, and the necklace to frame Jack.

And I was starting to have a sneaky feeling that I knew who.

Chapter 21

That night, I decided we should switch things up. I knew it wasn't all that safe for Jack to be out and about, but I wanted the nightly meeting out at our place. I wanted Liz in on it.

It was becoming more than plain that her manuscripts were the key to figuring this whole thing out, and leaving her out of the meeting, even if Jack couldn't see or hear her, just didn't seem right. Or smart. She would know the right questions to ask. At least I hoped so.

I even outdid myself and made Mom's famous little mini-meatloaves and homemade mashed potatoes. It took a lot of time peeling enough potatoes to feed a small horde like ours, but I did it and didn't complain once.

Mainly because the only ones I had to complain to were Liz, Destiny, and Yorkie Doodle, and none of them were in a position to be able to help me, anyway.

So, I took Destiny and Yorkie out for a short walk to check on the bunnies, who were doing fine, and then settled in at the kitchen counter to peel. At least I didn't have to worry about going to get Ruby tonight. Opal was dropping her off on her way to visit Mom. Seeing all the awesome furniture had Opal's brain working double time. They were going to start an inventory of sorts tonight.

Opal had even asked if I'd be interested in helping. But right now, my hands were more than full. So were Ruby's. I did offer to watch baby Pearl, though, so that Kimberly could go too. Opal had laughed at that. Her words were something along the lines of, "Your mother would be quite vexed at me if baby Pearl didn't show up with me."

Mason and Nancy got a lot of attention, don't get me wrong. But there was something about little Pearl that had suckered Mom and Opal in right from the very moment of her birth on All Hallows' Eve. I have to admit, she'd suckered me in too.

She was quite a cute and precious little baby. Being named after Grand didn't hurt, either.

By the time everyone was due to arrive, the potatoes were sitting all mashed and ready to eat and the timer was just about to go off for the meatloaves. I even had a large tray of rolls in the oven with the meatloaves. It might not be a seven-course meal, but there was meat and potatoes and bread. What more could anyone ever really ask for than that?

The only one I was really worried about pleasing was Lily. How wrong was that? But I knew her cooking was awesome. It worried me she might not think well of my abilities in the kitchen.

I broke off a small bite of one of the loaves and popped it in my mouth. To heck with that. They'd turned out perfect. If Lily had a problem with them, it was her problem alone. And there was always a bag of salad in the fridge if someone didn't like meatloaf at all. Jack came to mind there. I could totally see him thinking himself above a country meal like mine. I was okay with that. Pleasing him didn't concern me all that much.

Jack wasn't Lily. He wouldn't be in my life all that much longer.

"Do you think they'll like me? Have you told them about me, or am I to be a surprise?" Liz was leaning over my shoulder watching me give the loaves a last glaze of my special sauce.

"No, we haven't told them. And, come to think of it, you might want to stay out of sight until we have a chance to break it to them. If that's okay with you?"

She nodded. "That's cool." She stared at the food in front of her.

I had to ask. "Is it hard, not being able to eat?"

Liz thought about it for a minute, then shook her head. "No, not really. It would be different, I think, if I could smell it. But one has to be able to breathe to smell, and well, ghosts don't breathe. We don't have organs to do that kind of thing anymore."

"So it really doesn't bother you to watch us eat?" I'm thinking if I was a ghost, it would just about give me a second death. But then, I really love my food.

She smiled at me. "Not really, no. Do I wish I was still alive? Sure. But eating isn't one of the reasons at the top of the list."

As I said, Liz and I were very different people. Food would have been one of the very top items on my list. Top three for sure.

Arc and Ruby were the first to arrive, and they helped to set the table and get everything arranged. Then Lily's van pulled in and she, Merlin, and Jack got out and hurried inside. Not that anyone would see them way out here in the country, but I guess it paid to be safe.

Then again, the rush to get inside might have been due to the weather too. It was definitely cold out. Winter had officially arrived. Even if the calendar didn't agree with that yet.

Technically, as it was my house, I could have bypassed Lily's rule of no business discussion during dinner. But why mess with something that seems to work? Besides, we had more important things to discuss over dinner.

Mainly Liz.

We'd made it through most of dinner, though, before any of us figured out quite how to do this. As it was, Arc stepped up.

"Um, guys," Arc said, looking over at Merlin. "Have any of you ever heard that witches can see and communicate with ghosts?"

Lily, Merlin, and Jack looked at each other and then laughed. When the three of us didn't join in, they pulled themselves together. "Please don't tell me you think your house is haunted," Jack said with a smirk. "It's enough that you all expect me to believe in magic. Too much by far if you expect to add ghosts to that list."

"As much as I hate to say it, I have to go with Jack on this one," Merlin said. "Whatever it is that makes you think the place is haunted can be explained away by logic and science, I'm sure."

Now it was our turn to share a look.

"Oh, we don't think our house is haunted," I said.

Lily's shoulders fell. "Oh, good. You really had me worried there for a minute, dear."

"We don't think it's haunted, because we know it is."

Lily opened her mouth but Merlin put his hand on hers. "Perhaps you'd better explain."

"Actually, there's someone that can explain

things much better than we can," Ruby said. "Liz, you can come in now."

"Liz? Liz Jordan?" Jack shook his head. "This is so bogus."

Then Liz walked in. And Jack, the plain-Jane human that didn't believe in things like magic and ghosts, dropped his fork and let out a tiny scream.

I had expected Merlin and Lily to be able to see her, but Jack? Was he hiding even more from us than we knew?

Liz raised a hand and gave everyone a sad smile. "I'm friendly, I promise. Please don't freak out."

Jack's mouth opened and closed several times but nothing was coming out.

Lily stood and walked over to her. She held out a hand in front of her. "Do you mind, dear?"

Liz shook her head no, and Lily reached out to touch her arm. Only the hand didn't stop. "It's cold." Then Lily grimaced. "I'm sorry, dear, I mean you're cold."

"Most of the time, yeah. It's a ghost thing. But I can draw warmth to me too, if I need to."

Lily nodded. "That's nice dear."

I noticed that whenever Lily got nervous, she really overused the word dear. She was trying to act like this wasn't phasing her, but I could tell otherwise. She might have me beat when it came to acting skills, but she would not win any Oscars with this performance.

"Why don't you join us, Liz? We saved you a seat." Good thing I went for the big eight-seater table for family dinners, huh?

She tried hard to appear to be walking, and if you didn't look too closely, you could swear she was. Then she sat on the chair and folded her hands on the table. "Please don't let me disrupt your meal. Eat. And don't hesitate to ask me any questions you want to."

See, that's the whole reason we did it this way. We wanted to normalize Liz as much as we possibly could. Hard to do with a ghost, but we were trying. The hope was, the others would get their questions out in the open before our nightly meeting so that Liz could be a part of it.

But first, I had a question of my own.

"Before we get started, I have a question for Jack."

Jack started and looked at me. The man looked guilty as sin itself. "A question for me?"

I nodded. "Yup. You've been holding out on us, and frankly, I'm tired of it."

"Not this again," Merlin said. "I've told you, Amie, if there is something you need to know about the case that will help, Jack has sworn to me he'll tell you. And I believe him."

"Actually, my question isn't about the case. It's about Jack being a witch."

Lily and Merlin laughed. "He doesn't even believe in witches, dear," Lily said. "No way could he actually be one."

Only Jack wasn't laughing. The cat, or rather ghost, was already out of the bag. And he knew it.

When the two older witches finally caught onto Jack's silence, the laughter stopped. Merlin stared at Jack.

"Jack?"

"Look, I can explain," he said.

Lily shook her head. "No need for explanations, I think. It's pretty obvious why you are a witch in hiding. The council takes a very dim view of using magic for illegal purposes. And right now, I'm believing I know why you've had such a stellar career."

Lily always was a smart cookie.

Merlin's eyes widened. "Oh my Goddess, Jack!

Do you not know how bad this is?"

"Why do you think I've hidden it all these years? Even from my only real friends in the world? Kind of hard to do when you're as proud of it as I am," Jack said. Then he looked at me. "It was going great too. Until you got these kids involved in everything."

"Excuse me, but us 'kids' got involved when we took on a bounty hunting case, thank you very much." I glanced over at Merlin and Lily. "Is there a way to break all the current spells in a room?"

Lily frowned at me. "I believe so, but why do you ask?"

My eyes were back on Jack. "Because I've been wondering for quite some time why you two are friends with someone like Jack. It just makes little sense to me. You all are very different people. Not the kind that generally form life-long friendships."

Merlin shook his head at me. "Jack might have hidden his magic from us, but he wouldn't…" Then he looked over at Jack, who was looking guiltier by the minute. I wouldn't have thought that possible.

Jack, the overbearing, overconfident, British thief deflated right before our eyes. If I hadn't known any better, I have sworn the man before us now was a totally different Jack.

"I'm sorry." Jack stood. "I believe I know where this is going. I've done bad things, but I don't count making you two my friends as one of them. It might have been sneaky and underhanded, but I wanted you to like me as much as I liked you."

He looked over at me. "I think I'm ready for you to turn me in now."

Lily and Merlin shared a glance. "Not so fast. Sit down, Jack. We have things to discuss. First, I think it would be a very prudent thing to dispel all active spells in the room. Then we can see where we stand."

Sounded good to me. I didn't like the idea of Jack manipulating my new to me family with his hidden magic.

I wanted to know where we really stood.

And if Jack was as innocent as he said he was on this one. Right now, I wasn't so sure that was the case.

Chapter 22

It was shaping up to be another late night. Merlin ended up calling in Opal, so she stopped by on her way home with all the ingredients we needed for the dispel-all spell. Good thing Mom had a storehouse of magical properties.

The spell itself didn't take all that long. When it was over, Opal looked deep into Merlin and Lily's eyes. "Well?" she asked. "Either of you feel any differently toward Jack here?"

Merlin looked over at Jack and blew out a breath. "Not really. I still consider him a friend, even though I do find that I want to throttle him right now." He smiled. "In other words, nothing much has changed."

"Lily?" Jack asked, his voice holding a slight tremor.

She considered for a minute longer, taking her own sweet time about it. Finally, she shook her head. "About the same as Merlin, I think." Then her eyes narrowed as she glared at Jack. "But if you ever cast a spell on either of us again, friend or not, I will end you."

Jack swallowed and nodded. I believe he realized that a threat from Lily was a threat indeed. I know I did.

It was almost nine o'clock before we even started what was supposed to be the focus of the evening. Jack's case.

"Now that everybody is thinking and feeling with their own minds and emotions," I said. "Do you two still think Jack didn't take the necklace?"

Merlin nodded. "Yes, I still believe him. If for no other reason than he wouldn't have been foolish enough to let the police search his home with the piece sitting there in his jacket pocket. He might be sneaky and underhanded, but he isn't stupid."

"Okay, then. I think we all need to acknowledge that Jack's case and the disappearance of Liz's manuscripts are linked. That's pretty obvious what with Jack being the one to steal the hard copies. I'll even go so far as to say that I think the one framing him is the buyer for that job," I said.

"But why on earth would they wait until now? He stole that box years ago. What's changed?" Ruby asked.

"Well, in the spirit of turning over a new, more honest, leaf with you all, I have a confession to make," Jack said. "I peeked at what was in the box."

We all looked at him. "And?" I prompted.

"And there were three bound manuscripts inside. The first one was titled 'The Downing of Air Force One'."

Ruby's eyes widened. "I've read that book! Mabel recommended it to me. It just made the New York Times Bestseller list!"

Liz started jumping up and down. "It did?

Really? That's so awesome!"

Someone stole her life's work and was making a ton of money from it, and she thought it was awesome? That wouldn't be the word I'd use to describe it. At all.

Jack nodded. "It did. And I just heard that they have bought the rights to make a movie out of it…"

Whatever else Jack was going to say was lost in Liz's squeal of delight. "A movie! That's so cool." Then she got quiet. "But then I'll never be able to see it will I?"

Lily looked thoughtful. "Don't give up hope on that quite yet, dear. I have an idea that I'll work on for you."

Liz grinned at her. "Thanks."

And just like that, we lost Liz. She was far too excited to stay focused on the conversation at that point.

As she danced off, I turned to Jack. "So, if I'm getting your intention here right, you think whoever hired out that gig is now afraid that you did indeed peek and will cause problems for them?"

He nodded. "I'm not sure what they think I could do, actually, but yes, that's what I think."

I nodded. "I think so too." I looked at the others. "Anybody else think differently?"

There were a lot of shaking heads, but none nodding.

"Then I'm pretty sure I know who's behind all this. And I think maybe I know how we can catch her."

"Who?" Merlin asked, but Ruby and Arc's eyes met mine. They were right there with me. They just might make good partners after all.

"Well, there's only one person besides Liz who knew what those books were. Who had actually read them and could cause issues if someone tried to pass the work off as their own."

Merlin and Lily's eyes cleared. "Her agent."

And if she hadn't stopped at just the theft part, I'd dang well prove that too.

***

The plan was a simple one. All it really took was a phone call from me to set it into motion. The rest was up to Alice. If we were wrong, we'd all know it for a certainty within a couple of days. If we were right, we'd have Alice dead to rights.

I waited until I was sure the agency was open before making the call. Even then, I didn't get through. The agency hadn't seemed to be all that busy when I'd visited it days ago, but I was betting Alice was using her phone system to make it appear as though it was. Appearance is everything in some circles.

My impression was given even more solidity when she called back not five minutes later.

"This is Alice Mayfield. You called about Liz's manuscripts?" Her voice was breathless like she'd been running. Or maybe crying?

"Yes, I was in your office the other day, and I think I might have great news for you. I think I've found a copy of Liz's books."

There was a moment's silence. Then, "You have?" There was a definite squeak to her voice. She was so the one behind all this.

"I'm not one hundred percent certain yet, but yes, I think so. I paid a visit to Liz's brother Kyle after I stopped by your office."

"But I checked with him years ago. He doesn't have a copy." Her voice was gaining a little more confidence now. Time to knock that down a bit.

"You're right, he doesn't. But if you know Kyle at all, you know he's greedy as all get out." I paused to let that sink in. That was our main selling point for the story. "Well, Kyle knew that Liz had a ton of photos on her hard drive and that no way had she already sold them all, so he stood to make some money with them. He copied her hard drive files onto thumb drives and gave the drives to a friend of his to go through. According to Kyle, she knows how to sell photos."

Another silence. Longer this time. "You think he didn't just copy photo files?"

"I know he didn't. He isn't all that computer savvy, and he was afraid he'd miss something, so he copied it all. Isn't that great?"

"Um, yeah. So, who is this friend of his again?"

We had her.

"A woman named Lily Hilton. She lives on the outskirts of Oak Hill. She's leaving this morning for a few days down in Indy, but she's agreed to meet with me with she comes back. I wanted to give you a head's up so you could start coming up with a plan to shop the books with some publishers. No need to wait, right?"

"Yeah, sure, right." She was quiet, and I might not be able to see the wheels turning in her brain, but I swear I could almost hear them. "Let me know when you have them, okay?"

"I promise, you'll be the first to know."

We ended the call, and I sat back. The plan was in motion now.

All we had to do was wait.

Chapter 23

I didn't get to rest on my laurels all that long before my cell phone went off. Glancing down at the screen, Mineheart Law beamed up at me. Hmm, that didn't narrow down the caller all that much. One of three.

Turns out it was Archie... Dad, that is.

"Hey, Dad, what's up?"

"I just got an interesting phone call that I thought you should know about."

"Oh? Who from?"

"Kyle Jordan's lawyer. He wants to back out of the contract."

Fat chance of that happening. I was pretty sure our lawyers could out-legal Kyle's seven days a week and twice on Sunday.

"You told him that wasn't going to happen, right?"

"I did. But he made me promise to ask all of you

to reconsider the deal. For what it's worth, Kyle is willing to reimburse you all for your moving and expenses to date."

I laughed. "How very generous of him. But no thanks. He just wants this place back because he hates Liz and doesn't want her to have friends."

There was silence. "But Liz is dead. Did I miss something?"

Ah, Merlin and Arc must not have shared the news yet. "Kind of. Liz is dead, yeah, but she hasn't exactly vacated the premises if you will. Turns out witches can see and talk to ghosts. Who knew?"

More silence. This time he didn't end it.

"No, I haven't lost my marbles. Not yet anyway. Ask Arc and Merlin, they've both spent some time with her. She's nice once you get past the whole haunting thing."

"I see. I'll definitely be talking to my brother about this. But about the other matter, I can relay to Kyle's attorney that the three of you are standing firm on your legal ground?"

"You can." I paused. "And anytime you and Mom want to come over and meet Liz, just say the word. She really is pretty awesome."

"We'll keep that in mind."

My phone started beeping and Opie's name and number flashed across the screen. "Sorry, Dad, but Opie's calling, and I need to take this. Talk to you soon."

Then I swiped the screen to accept Opie's call. No way did I want to miss this. He'd left a message on my phone last night that all was well, but we hadn't actually spoken. I was still worried about him. Missy, not so much, even if she was the one missing.

"Everything okay?"

He laughed. "Hello, and I love you too."

I felt the tension drain off me in waves. If he

was joking around, then the danger period had passed. He was okay.

"Sorry, my dearest love, Trevor Opie Taylor. How are you this fine and beautiful morning?"

"Wonderful, actually. We found Missy. I almost hate to say it, but as it turns out you and Van's dad were pretty right about her. She has a much darker side than the one she'd shown to me and the rest of the world."

"Did she hurt Van?"

"No, they're still together, but with some new rules in place...," he trailed off. "But that is actually a kind of long story, and I don't have much time right now. The plane's about to take off."

"The plane? I thought you guys drove?"

"We did, but I'm flying home to my girl. Can't stand to think about adding another two days to the journey." Two whole days? Where the heck was he, anyway? "I was kind of hoping you could pick me up from the airport? In about, oh, three hours or so?"

I nodded into the phone, then took down his flight number and information. "See you then. Fly safe, okay?"

"That's really up to the plane and the pilot, but sure, I'll do my best. Love you, Amie."

"Love you, Trevor." It took real effort on my part to use his given name, but it meant so much to him. I knew he had to be smiling as he ended the call.

***

You know all those totally cheesy movies where the girl or guy shows up at the airport with a big, embarrassing sign? Yeah, I totally did that. He deserved it, in more ways than one.

When he saw me holding it, he was instantly on board, running toward me and then sweeping me off my feet. There were a ton of phones focused on us by then, so I kind of figured we'd go viral on Facebook very shortly. That was okay with me. I loved my man, and I didn't care who knew it.

Even if he had dissed moving in day to provide security for an ex's wedding. I was trying hard not to think too much about that.

He was still laughing when he set me back down. "You really are something, you know that?"

I nodded. "Right back at you, dude." Then I paused. "Do you have luggage to pick up?"

"Nope, Dad's bringing it back in the car. We're good to go. I was kind of thinking your place if that's okay with you?"

Like that would be a problem. Although, I had some explaining to do before we got there. Or maybe, it would be better if I didn't? After all, he couldn't see or hear Liz. Would he even believe me?

Then again, if I started having conversations with thin air, he might start worrying about my sanity. Not that he wouldn't worry about it when I told him the house was haunted. But better to be honest and upfront about it.

As we walked out to the car, I pulled him in close and said, "Oh, by the way, the new place is haunted."

He glanced down at me, but never missed a step. That's my man. "I wondered why you guys got it so cheap. That would make sense." We took a few more steps. "Since you don't seem to be too upset about it, I'm taking it that the spirit is friendly?"

He might not have missed a step, but I stopped cold. "Wait a minute. Are you telling me you believe in ghosts?"

That got a frown. "Well, don't you? Otherwise, why did you just tell me the place was haunted?"

"Well, yeah, I believe now, but not before I met Liz."

His eyes widened. "You know who the ghost is? That's so cool."

It took that for me to remember what his all-time favorite movie in the whole wide world was. Ghostbusters. Of course, he believed in ghosts.

"Yeah, turns out witches can see and hear ghosts." He looked disappointed. "We'll see if we can figure out some way for you to see her too. I mean, they have equipment for that sort of thing now, don't they? Real stuff, I mean, not like in your movie."

"They do." His step had a bounce to it as we started walking again. "In fact, I think I know where I can borrow some from. Maybe we could set up a ghost hunt tomorrow?"

I hated to burst his bubble, but the next few days were kind of booked. "Might have to wait a day or two. I have a lot to catch you up on."

When we got to the car, he held out his hand for the keys. He was such a man. But I didn't argue. I just handed them over and got into the passenger side of the car.

As he drove, I started filling him in on everything that was going on. The only thing I left out was the fact that we knew exactly where the bond-jumping burglar was hiding out. At the end of the day, Opie was still the law. He believed we should follow it at all times. He'd made an exception to his rule for my half-brother, Arc. I didn't think we'd get one this time.

Not that I would blame Opie at all for that. Arc had been innocent. Innocent wasn't a word I would use to describe Jack. I could think of a fair few descriptive words for him, but innocent wasn't one of them.

We were out of the city and on the curvy country roads when I started to notice Opie's distraction.

"Am I boring you?"

"No," he drawled. "But this agent you told me about, do you think maybe she really did kill Liz?" He glanced in the rearview mirror yet again.

"I think it's a distinct possibility, yes. According to some research I've done on her, she came into quite a bit of money a couple of years ago. That money might well have come from selling Liz's books. And I'm not talking an agent's percentage, either."

He nodded. "That could be an incentive, then."

I glanced behind us. "What's so interesting back there?" All I saw was an old beat-up pickup truck. They were a dime a dozen out here in the country. Not all that unusual.

"Well, that pickup has been with us since we left the airport. I'm thinking maybe it was waiting there for us to leave."

"They're following us? Why?"

I glanced back just in time to see the pickup speed up.

"Whatever the reason, I think we're about to find out. Hang on." Opie stepped on the gas, but my little go mobile wasn't really built for speed. Good gas mileage and dependability, sure. Speed, no. She just didn't have the power to outrun the guy, or girl as the case may be, in the vehicle behind us.

I was still staring at the truck when I saw the gun come out of the window, pointed toward us. "Opie, gun!"

"Get down!" He swerved just as the bullets started flying. There was a loud bang like a mini-explosion, and then the car went wild. It didn't take a rocket scientist to figure out that we now had three tires instead of two.

Opie stepped briefly on the gas, the polar opposite of what I would have done, and then just held on. As the road we were currently traveling on had steep drop-offs on either side, I was so thankful he had the wheel. I suspect that things would have ended very differently if I'd have made an issue about handing over the keys.

As he was trying to keep control, the pickup sped up and swerved past us, barely missing my car as it listed to the left, right toward the steepest part of the drop-off.

If we could just make it another quarter mile, the road would level out with the ground and we'd be okay.

The only problem was, time itself seemed to be slowing down.

Chapter 24

We made it. Even my little green baby.

Opie held it on the road, and eventually, we made it to a stop. Of course, we were still in the middle of the road, so we weren't exactly in the clear.

As soon as the car was at a full stop, he shut it off and turned on the blinkers. Then he jumped out and opened the trunk. Within seconds, he had the little bright orange triangles up to warn oncoming traffic. I was appreciating his taste in Christmas gifts a little more now. Not something I would have bought for myself, for sure.

It took a while for Opie to change the tire, and I stood there with my hand in my pocket the entire time. There was a reason for that. I wasn't willing to let my taser out of my hand, and we didn't want to freak out passers-by. But we also wanted to be ready in case the pickup doubled back to finish the job.

Not that a taser would hold up against an actual

firearm. But we could duck behind the car if bullets started flying. I was hoping she'd be motivated enough to get out and come after us. Close enough for the taser to do its job.

"Don't suppose you got a look at the driver?" I asked.

"Afraid I was a bit busy at the time. You?"

"Nope. All I saw was a bunch of red hair. I'm pretty sure it was a wig."

"That seems to be a safe bet." Opie stood up to put the tire changing tools away. "Get in. I want to drive it a way and pull off someplace safe to see if there's any other damage before we go much farther."

Thank the Goddess, there wasn't. The only damage was to the tire and rim. It could have been so much worse. If I'd been driving, it would have been.

I really wanted to have a long talk with Ms. Mayfield.

The rest of the drive was a silent one. Each of us lost in our own thoughts. Opie headed straight for the new house. Once we were inside, we called everyone to let them know what had happened. Needless to say, our calls didn't make anyone very happy.

We really hadn't thought that Ms. Mayfield would make a move until after dark, and we also really hadn't thought she'd come after one of us. We'd kind of thought she'd just go after the proof. The thumb drives.

That, we had been ready for. Arc and Ruby were already camped out at Lily's. I'd have been there too, but Opie came first. Plus, the whole burglars tend to work at night thing.

The reasons we'd put such a time limit on the open window to take the non-existent drives from Lily's were two-fold. First, we wanted her to hit while we were prepared and ready for her. Well, that part had massively failed when she changed the game on us.

But second, we wanted her to be desperate enough to do the job herself. According to Jack, it would be impossible to set up a gig with the broker in such a short time. If someone came calling in the middle of the night, chances were very good it would be Alice herself.

And she would find us right there waiting for her.

***

Opie and I spent a few hours at the house, so he could get a feel for the place—and Liz—and we could both unwind a little. We needed it.

A few boxes got unpacked, introductions were made, even if they were a little one-sided, and yes, we spent a little time cuddling. We needed that too. I'd missed my man, and by the looks of it, he'd missed me too. Missy or no Missy.

Around three, we headed over to Lily's via a very roundabout route. We didn't know how or when she'd case the joint, as they say, but we were pretty sure she would. That meant we couldn't very well go in the front door without the possibility of being seen and her knowing it was a trap.

So we dressed up in our little disguises and parked three entire blocks away. You might not think that sounds like a lot. But as cold as it was, it sure felt like a lot. I pulled my scarf tighter as we walked to keep my nose from freezing off my face. It worked to a point, but not like sitting home with the furnace cranked up. Once we caught Alice in the act and got everything squared away with Jack and the bond, it might be time to try out my new fireplace. I'd never had one of those before. I was looking forward to the romantic possibilities.

Which reminded me, I needed to get a soft fluffy

rug to go on the floor in front of it. Come to think of it, I'd seen one in Mom and Dad's attic. Hopefully, Opal hadn't snatched it up yet. I'd definitely be going back for that.

By the time we made it to Lily's back door, the others that were coming were already pretty much in place. We'd tried to talk Jack out of coming, but that hadn't really worked out. His choice of disguise made me laugh though.

Jack might make a fairly striking man, but as a woman, he fell far short. Especially with the long, flowing dress and black tights he'd chosen. Where on earth did he get the outfit, anyway? I was pretty sure Merlin didn't keep women's clothes lying around his house. Unless, of course, they were Lily's and this get-up didn't look at all like something she'd wear. Or be caught dead in.

Working as a team, we finished up getting the place ready for the night's activities. I already knew that Lily's place was well-guarded by the Mineheart Fireworks Ward. We'd had to find a way to temporarily disarm that. That little project was all Merlin and Arc. They were the resident experts on the warding.

Opie and I were in charge of surveillance equipment. It amazed me that Lily had so much to offer. There wasn't much to really set up, all we had to do was move things around a bit to take advantage of what she had. We wanted the evening's activities to be caught on tape for all the world to see.

"You know this probably won't end the way you want it to," Opie said as we angled yet another camera to catch more of the office area. "I don't want you to have your heart set on everything wrapping up nicely tonight."

I just looked at him. "What do you mean? If we catch her trying to steal a thumb drive of Liz's manuscripts, it pretty much nails her, doesn't it?"

He hesitated. "For breaking and entering, yes. For attempted burglary, yes. For anything else, not really. You still have no proof that she stole Liz's manuscripts nor that she profited off of them." Another pause. "We also have no proof that she set Jack up, you know. I don't think a judge and jury would really take into account the hearsay testimony of a phone call with a criminal broker."

I stared at him in horror. "Then all this is for nothing?"

Opie waggled his head back and forth. "That's a possibility, yes. I mean, if she shows up, it will be bad for her. Just probably not as bad as you think. Unless..." He glanced around at all the equipment.

"Unless what?"

"Unless we can get her to confess. If we get a full confession on video, that would go a long way to freeing Jack and seeing justice done for Liz." He looked straight into my eyes. "If I'm reading between the lines correctly, you think she killed Liz, don't you?"

I nodded. "Yeah, I do. And of all the things I want to nail her on, that one's the most important."

He gathered me into a hug and kissed the top of my head. "I know."

"Got any ideas how we get a confession out of her?"

He took a deep breath and shook his head. "No, but I'm working on it. If I come out with something crazy, just go with me, okay?"

"You got it."

Normally, I hated Daylight Savings Time, but right at this moment, I was a big fan of it. I wanted dark to fall early so we could get this show on the road.

Around seven o'clock, it was just about as dark as it would get. We even got lucky. The moon was only a small sliver in the dark night's sky. Not enough to give a would-be burglar pause.

Lily had one camera set up at the back of her mailbox pointing toward the house. If Alice came in the front, we'd see her coming. We even made it easy for her. The key to the front door was sitting on the frame above the door. If she looked hard enough, she'd find it. If not, then we'd see just what she had up her sleeve. I was hoping that whatever it was, it wouldn't cause too much damage.

We were all sitting quietly in the dark in different rooms of the downstairs of the house, waiting. About seven-thirty, the fun started.

Alice arrived.

Chapter 25

We watched her on the camera as she looked first under the little welcome mat, then under the flowerpots, and finally, when we'd almost given up that we'd hidden the key a little too well, she ran her fingers around the door frame.

As one of the ones stationed in the main living room the front door led into, I could hear her soft "Yes!" through the door.

It was me, Opie, and Lily in this room. The others would join pretty quickly once we gave the word. But we didn't want to go too quickly. We wanted her on tape, or actually virtual tape, searching the house. We didn't want to take any chances. And we wanted her really uptight and nervous when we finally stepped up and showed ourselves. I kind of figured the longer she was there, the more nervous she'd become.

Jack had helped out with one of his stealth

spells. All of us were ducked behind furniture as it was, but with the spell that made Jack such a great burglar, we were practically invisible—even to each other. I would learn that spell. Whether Jack wanted to teach it to me or not. He owed me.

Alice came in the front door and immediately locked it behind her, then glanced out the window to see if anyone had noticed her entry. Once she was satisfied that she was in the clear, she turned and looked around the room. She took out a small penlight and flashed it around. We'd left the office door open, kind of tempting her to go inside.

She did.

We followed. And yes, we each had Ruby's quiet shoes spell firmly in place. Alice wouldn't just not see us; she wouldn't hear us either.

As we watched, she started going through the desk drawers, mumbling to herself. "Be here, be here... yes!"

The yes was when she found the thumb drive in the middle left-hand drawer. We'd even gone so far as to put it in an envelope with 'Property of Kyle Jordan' written on the outside. We didn't want to take any chances.

Once she had slid the large envelope—we'd even included some nature photos to sell it even further—into the satchel she carried, she turned toward the door back into the living area.

That's when we dropped our spells.

She wasn't happy to find herself surrounded. "What the..." she trailed off, even as the tears started. "No, this can't be, it just can't end like this."

Alice reached into her purse, and Arc tackled her from behind. In his defense, we kind of all thought she was going for a gun. Especially after our little run-in with her in the pickup truck this afternoon. But no gun.

Just tissues.

Once we got that all straightened out, Alice sat there on the floor crying. We all just looked at each other. This wasn't quite the cold-blooded killer we'd all been expecting.

Finally, her eyes searched me out. "There was never any proof of Liz's manuscripts, was there?"

I shook my head. "No, they are well and truly gone. You and Kyle made a good team making sure of that."

She grimaced. "Please don't speak of me and Kyle as a team. We are anything but. I knew what he'd do with those books, and I just couldn't stand the thought of them being lost forever." She blew her nose and then squared her shoulders. "And I'd do it again, too. If I hadn't, then I'd have been faced with two options. One, the world would never see Liz's books which was absolutely a horrid thought. Or two, Kyle would end up profiting from them and taking credit for them himself. Somehow that was even worse."

"I have to ask, though," Jack said stepping into the light. "Why on earth did you try to frame me for taking that blasted necklace?"

She blinked at him. Then recognition slowly came. "You're Jack Watson?" She shook her head. "I'm afraid I will not apologize to you. I've read the papers, and you are a burglar plain and simple. Celeste is a friend of mine."

He blew out a breath. "I wish to bloody heck and back that I'd never heard of Bonsai."

"I know your reputation, and I know you looked inside that box. Maybe even read one of them. They are kind of addictive. From there, it would only be a matter of time for you to run across the books, especially once they hit the big screen, and start trying to find me for blackmail."

Jack straightened. "I'll have you know, dear lady, that I am a burglar, not a blackmailer. I find that very thought reprehensible."

Good to know he drew a line somewhere, but we were getting off-topic. And I was getting anxious. I didn't just want Alice on minor charges.

"Okay, so I have to ask. Why did Liz have to die?"

Alice's eyes snapped to mine in a heartbeat. "I didn't kill her for the books, if that's what you are insinuating. I would never have hurt Liz. She was my friend." The crying started again. "She believed in me. No one else seems to."

Crapsnackles. Had I really gotten it wrong? All of this, and Liz's death really was an accident?

It was beginning to look that way. Then again...

"If that's true, then why did you shoot out my tire this afternoon?"

She tilted her head at me. "What the bloody dickens are you talking about? Yes, I arranged to have the manuscripts stolen. Yes, I tried to frame Jack for taking that hideous necklace. But that's it. I didn't hurt Liz, and I most certainly didn't shoot out your tire. I don't even own a gun!"

I looked over at Opie. I wasn't sure I believed her, but maybe we had our bad guys mixed up. Maybe whoever had shot out that tire hadn't been after me at all. Maybe they'd been after Opie.

"Could someone from your last... job... have followed you home?" I asked.

He shook his head. "I don't see how. We tied up all the loose strings nice and tight." Then he hesitated. "Unless we missed one somewhere."

As worrying as that thought was, we had other things to take care of now.

I had been afraid that Jack would go back on his

word to let us turn him in when the time came. But he didn't. We took him and Alice and turned them both in, with video documentation of her confession. It should be a simple case of transferring the guilt from Jack to Alice.

Once the appropriate people viewed the video—and yes, we made copies beforehand—he should be free to go back to his old life of crime. Even better, I wouldn't have to see him again. I don't know why, but I just didn't trust the man. Especially now that I know he was a witch in hiding. The council was scary, but they served a purpose.

And that purpose was to keep people like Jack from using magic for evil intents and purposes. Hopefully, Merlin and Lily could make him see the light on that point. If not? Well, I might just be seeing Jack again after all.

It would be the next day before we could turn in the paperwork and get our measly small bounty. Which, of course, would immediately be turned over to pay back Merlin. The plus was that we should also be picking up that bigger case file. The one that would give us a big jump on that balloon payment in a year's time. Now that we didn't have to buy furniture for the houses, it would go a lot further toward just that.

By the time we all made it back home, it was the early hours of the morning. Opie didn't go back on duty for another two days, and I planned to make the most of them.

I'd missed him, and we would spend part of that time cuddling and talking. But we would spend even more time unpacking and getting things arranged just the way I wanted them.

We were lying in bed, all snuggled together when he broached the subject of moving in. I'd been biting my tongue on that very subject for a while now.

"I've been thinking. If you're serious about us

taking this to the next level, I'd be willing to move in here. On a trial basis. I could move some of my stuff over and maybe start out with a couple nights a week? See how it goes?"

I smiled and snuggled in deeper. My man made a very good snuggle bunny. "That sounds good to me. We could start now, right?"

He chuckled. "Sounds good to me."

With that settled, I started to drift off. Tomorrow, there would be more to do than just cuddle and unpack. There were wards to set up too. Even as I drifted off, I wondered if there was a way to ward a car. Might not be a bad idea.

Destiny woke me up around three o'clock... in the morning. It was still dark, and we couldn't have been asleep for more than thirty minutes. To say I wasn't happy was a vast understatement. At least until she told me why.

"There's someone in the house. Someone bad. You need to prepare."

Chapter 26

I punched Opie to wake him up. "Someone's in the house."

My man didn't question how I knew. He just reacted. The first thing he did was reach for the nightstand by the bed. That's where his pistol normally rested as he slept. Only this time, because of airport security measures, he didn't have it with him. At this point, it was probably traveling slowly back home in the sheriff's trunk.

"Crap." He looked over at me. "Lock yourself in the bathroom and dial 9-1-1. I'll take care of this."

I shook my head even as I was digging in my closet for my baseball bat. I'd brought it over for home security in one of my very first boxes.

"It's Kyle. And he's got a gun." A frantic Liz floated through our partially opened bedroom door. "I think he's totally lost it this time! What are we going to do?"

Well, for starters, the baseball bat would not do us any good. Opie beat me to my pack with the taser. "Bathroom now."

I just looked at him and raised my hands. My hair started its flowing thing as the magic began pouring into me. "Without your firearm, I'm the more dangerous of the two of us, you know. You get in the damn bathroom yourself."

We had a minute-long stare down, but neither of us was giving. "Guys, he's coming up the stairs. Do something."

I picked up the bat again and got behind the door. It was worth a shot. If he would just come in far enough.

He didn't.

Kyle stopped in the doorway. His pistol aimed at Opie. "I'd drop that taser if I were you. You might get the shot off, but you'd be dead before the working end ever came close to me." He paused, grinning madly. "And tell your girlfriend to come out from behind the door with that bat. I'm not that dumb."

How did he know? Then I remembered the old adage, if you can see someone in a mirror, like the dresser mirror I was using to keep tabs on Kyle, then they could see you.

Crapsnackles.

When Opie still seemed to be debating firing the taser, Kyle shifted the gun to the door. A bullet would have no trouble getting through the thin wood and into me. That changed things, and Kyle had known it would.

Personally, I was kind of grateful for Kyle's move, even though it put me in imminent danger. I could totally see Opie sacrificing himself if he thought he could take down Kyle and save the rest of us. And I really didn't want that happening.

A life without Opie just wouldn't be worth living.

Opie lowered the taser, and I came around the side of the door to stand beside him. That was when I got my first real good look at Kyle. Liz was right. He'd rounded the bend into madness.

Even as I looked at him, he broke out in a shiver. "Tell my damn sister to stay the hell away from me."

My eyes met Liz's, and she gave me a pleading look. She wanted to help, but how could a ghost help us now?

"You want this place back that badly?" I asked. "What, did you find out it was built on a hidden vault of gold or something?"

He laughed. "As if you don't know. I've done my research on witches. One of my platoon in the service was a witch. It almost drove the man mad when members of our squad were killed in an enemy raid. He said their ghosts wouldn't leave him alone. They all had messages for him to take back home." He paused. "I should have researched the three of you better before selling this place to you. But who would have thought you'd all be witches? You don't wear those stupid pointed hats or anything."

Kyle stepped in and to the side, then motioned with the end of the gun for us to go through the doorway. "After you," he said. "The others might grow impatient if we take too long joining them."

So much for hoping that the others would come to rescue us. He must have started at the barn and then worked his way to the house. We so should have made the house wards a bigger priority. Note to future self, that. If there was a future self past tonight.

Opie and I walked hand in hand down the stairs. Kyle was following too closely behind for us to actually say anything to each other. So I reached out to someone else.

"Destiny? Any bright ideas on how to handle this? Please tell me you have a plan."

"I'm going after Yorkie and Baxter. Hopefully, we can come up with something. Just stay alive until we do. Remember, the Goddess has big plans for the three of you. Don't go spoiling them now."

I swallowed. Looked like we were pretty much on our own. I didn't see how two cats and a tiny dog could save us. But then again, they were very special animals. Maybe there was a chance after all.

As we came off the stairs, I saw Ruby and Arc all trussed up on back-to-back kitchen chairs. Gun or no gun, I ran to them and yanked the gags out of their mouths.

That was all Kyle gave me the time to do before he shoved me hard to the side. "Gags are okay. Out here in the middle of nowhere, there isn't anyone to hear you all scream, anyway." The grin on his face was hideous. "That means I can take my time with you all. That makes me happy."

Usually, I raised my hands to direct my magic, but somehow, I knew that wasn't an option this time. I'd have to rely on mental control alone. Good thing I'd kept up on practicing just that.

When my hair started floating, though, he raised the gun level to my head. "Oh, don't even think about it. I've taken precautions against your evil magic." He jerked his head at Ruby. "Just ask your cousin there."

Ruby swallowed and nodded. "Don't try it, Amie. He's shielded himself somehow. The magic bounces back." She glared at him. "It's how he got us. We took ourselves down with our own magic."

Okay, so that was very good to know. And very scary too. If we didn't have our magic, and we didn't have a gun, then what on earth did we have. Besides two cats and a dog, that is.

Either Kyle had left the front door partially open, or the animals had another way to access the house. I caught movement out of the corner of my eye. Destiny was slinking up behind Kyle.

"He's shielded by magic," Destiny beamed to me. "But he isn't shielded from harm. Your grand's levitation spell."

That just might work.

Kyle jerked as the tall lamp in the corner of the room moved on its own accord. Or at least it seemed to. His eyes grew wild.

"Tell her to stop it. Now, or I swear I'll shoot."

I tried to stay calm, after all, the gun was still pointing in my general direction. If he totally lost it, I'd be the first to go. And the others wouldn't have all that much hope after that.

"You think I have control over your sister? Why is she so pissed at you, Kyle?"

"Oh, drop the act. I know she's told you by now. Probably blabbed everything that happened that night."

"You mean the night you killed her?" Ruby said from behind him. "Actually, she hadn't mentioned it. She said she couldn't remember anything about that night."

He laughed. "Well, then this is a little anti-climactic, isn't it?" His laughter grew. "Guess I can just let you all go and go on home, now, can't I?"

So very far around that bend. I truly doubted at this point that Kyle would ever be able to pass as normal again.

The levitation spell had its limits, and I was searching for an object light enough to move that would be heavy enough to do damage to, oh, say Kyle's skull. I wished I'd taken the time to do more unpacking. Only the heavy stuff was out in the open here.

I was running out of options.

Then I remembered back to that fateful night in the back of Opal's shop. The night I'd almost gone around the bend myself when Naomi Hill had tried to kill my family.

Naomi had a gun too. Hadn't worked out for her, though. Not after Ruby super-heated the gun and made her drop it. That hadn't stopped the dang thing from going off and crippling my man for weeks on end.

Not exactly something I wanted to repeat.

I thought back to the gun safety classes Opie had made me take back in the days when I was considering getting a firearm of my own. Before I came into my magic. Now, I'm my own firearm. And I have two of them. Arms that is.

Sorry, my mind tends to take weird paths when under duress. Like, you know, standing in a room with your family and loved ones with a madman holding a gun.

Back to the safety classes. It was very important not to obstruct the barrel of the gun. Doing so would create a massive problem, and very likely end up with the firearm exploding in your hand.

Sounded good to me right now.

I stared hard at the end of that barrel and pushed a little heat to it. Not a lot at first. I had no way of knowing if the shield that was protecting Kyle was also protecting his gun. If it was, the very last thing I wanted to do was catch myself on fire.

Ruby must have noticed my intense concentration. She knew me well enough to know that I wouldn't wait too long to make some kind of move. Not with these stakes.

"Just out of curiosity," Ruby said. "How did you manage to make our magic double back on us? Are you a warlock or something?"

He spared her a darting glance, then his eyes focused back on me. Well, she had tried.

"No, I'm not a warlock. Thank the lord. At the very least, it spared me all the rantings and ravings of my lunatic sister after she died."

"I'm the lunatic?" Liz screeched and then attacked him. Unfortunately, none of her punches or kicks did anything more than make him shiver a bit.

"Although I do wish I'd just taken the extra step and had her exorcised or something. That will be my next step, trust me." He looked around. "Always did like this place. It'll be nice living here once I get rid of all the obstacles."

No heat had returned to me, so I doubled down and forced a massive wave of heat directly into the barrel of that firearm. I realized it was working when I saw the metal start to sort of... well... bubble.

I was kind of surprised Kyle didn't react to the extra heat. I knew I was concentrating on the barrel, but surely some heat was traveling up that pistol. But then again, he most likely thought it was Liz up to her tricks.

Boy, would he be surprised.

"Now!" Destiny beamed. I'll never be quite sure if she was talking to me, or just to the other familiars, but several things happened in close sequence.

Yorkie Doodle flew into the room and attacked Kyle's ankles with a vigor I'd never seen in the little dog to date. Destiny took a mighty leap and landed with all the force she could muster on his back, then proceeded to climb her way up and on top of his head. And lastly, Baxter positioned herself squarely beside Kyle's feet.

With the sudden onset of the familiars' attack, he stumbled just an inch or so to the right, meeting with a very solid cat's body. It was enough to throw him off balance, and he landed hard.

Unfortunately, he had been trained well. Even as

he landed, he was twisting his body into a firing position. The gun now leveled at Opie.

Opie took me to the floor, and things almost went very badly because of it. I almost missed Yorkie Doodle's next move, which was to change his focus from Kyle's ankles to his gun-holding hand.

"No, Yorkie!" I yelled, and I pushed more magic than I should have at the poor little dog who was doing his level best to save us all. His little furry body flew through the air and didn't stop until it hit the sofa behind him.

"What the..." Ruby yelled.

If she finished that statement, no one knew, because it was at that precise moment that Kyle pulled the trigger.

Chapter 27

The explosion might have been a small one, but it was loud enough to hurt my ears. The barrel of the gun gave way and Kyle screamed out in pain, clutching his right hand with his left.

The gun landed at his feet. Not that it would do anyone any good after this. It was far beyond repair.

Opie moved fast. Especially for a man wearing only silk boxer shorts. Something that I hadn't had the brainpower to recognize until now.

Within seconds, Kyle was trussed up, and Opie was looking at me. "He's going to need an ambulance."

I nodded and started to run upstairs for my phone. I say I started because that's when I noticed the flashing red and blue lights coming through the thin curtains and heard several vehicles screeching to a halt outside.

We all looked at each other.

"Did you have time to call them before he got to you?" I asked Ruby.

She just shook her head. "I thought maybe you had."

The front door flew open and there stood Opal, with two rather large sheriff's deputies standing behind her with their guns drawn. Of the three of them, Opal was the scariest by far. Guns or no guns.

Opie held his hands up, showing that he wasn't the one causing the trouble here. It took a few minutes to update them on what had happened, and for them to get Kyle loaded up in the waiting ambulance.

As it turned out, Opal had been awake when our protection gems on our bracelets had gone off. The first thing she'd done was call for an ambulance and the police to our address. The second thing she'd done was hightail it over here herself.

It's always good to have the cavalry waiting on the sidelines to come to your rescue. And you can't beat the Ravenswind family when it came to the cavalry.

The ambulance hadn't even made it out of the drive before Mom, Archie, Merlin, and Lily showed up. They arrived roughly at the same time. As I said, you can't beat my family when it comes to whole-scale rescues. Though I might have to stretch it to include the Minehearts and Lily too.

One deputy had stuck around after seeing the other one off with Kyle in the ambulance. Now, he was busy taking down statements. But his eyes kept going back to the barrel of that very damaged gun.

Finally, he closed his notebook and looked up at me. "I don't suppose you'd be willing to tell me how you managed to destroy the man's firearm?"

Before I could come up with any kind of response, Lily laughed, drawing his attention to her.

"That's a trade secret, I'm afraid. By now, you probably realize we're witches, dear. We're very good at keeping secrets. We have to be."

An odd expression crossed his face, but he left it at that and then he left to join his partner at the hospital.

Good thing too, because my mind had switched to other things that were demanding answers. Lily's words had rung off a warning bell inside my head. I'd heard those words almost verbatim not all that long ago. Over a phone call.

My horrified stare must have gotten the hairs on the back of her neck going straight up, because she turned to look at me. I could see by the widening of her eyes, that too late she realized she had given away her entire secret identity. And now she was afraid I would spill it out to the others.

She held her hand out to me. "Come, dear," she said. "I think maybe we owe this heroic little puppy a nice walk."

I glanced down at Yorkie Doodle who luckily looked none the worse for wear. As always with the mention of the word walk, he was ready to go.

"Sure," I said slowly. Then I looked up at Opie and the others. "Lily and I are going to go out for a breath of air. We'll be back soon, okay?"

They all nodded, distractedly. Between Liz, Ruby, Arc, and Opie, they'd catch the others up to date without me. In fact, they didn't even really notice when we left. Well, none of them but Opie noticed, anyway. He pulled me to one side and kissed the top of my side.

"Great thinking, kiddo. I don't know why I ever doubt you anymore."

I hugged him tight and gave him a quick peck on the lips. "Just remember those words, love. Not that I'll ever let you forget them."

He grinned at me, nodded at Lily, and went back

to the others. He might not know why, but he recognized the fact that Lily and I wanted to be alone. The others were far too distracted by recent events. It was probably better that way.

She waited until we were out of earshot of the house and those inside. "It was the whole secret speech, wasn't it?"

I nodded. "Yeah. Almost word for word."

"I realized that a little too late." She hesitated, and we watched as Yorkie investigated a small bush. "So, will you be telling the others?"

"I don't like keeping secrets from my family, you know."

She nodded. "I know, and I respect that. But this isn't exactly your secret to share, now is it?"

"Did you mean what you said that night? About not taking any more jobs that could actually hurt people?"

"Yes." She slowed to a stop and turned to look at me, her eyes meeting mine directly. "You gave me a lot to think about that night, you know. I've rather changed how I do things now. It might cut my business in half, but I'm okay with that."

I took a deep breath. "Well, then. I guess there isn't any need to bring the others into it, then is there?" I mean, it wasn't like we would turn in Merlin's gal to the law. She was the next best thing to family, herself.

Lily closed her eyes and raised her face to the heavens. "Thank you, Goddess," she whispered.

Destiny, at her feet, meowed.

***

The sun was up before we finally made it back to bed. I was very thankful that neither of us had anywhere to be the next day, as we slept in until noon.

We probably would have slept longer, if it hadn't been for the pounding on the door.

I opened it and stared directly into Patricia Bluespring's cold green eyes. "What?"

"Is it true? Kyle really killed poor Liz?" She glanced behind me, and I felt the chill at my back. I'd let Liz answer this one. Once Kyle had confessed his crime, her memories of that night had unlocked, showing the despicable coward in action.

"I'm going back to bed. You and Liz can talk this out." Then, after two short steps, I turned back to Liz. "Wait a minute. If you were stuck here because of unfinished business—being that you were actually murdered and all—shouldn't you have crossed over when we solved that?"

She looked at me and then ducked her head. "Well, the light showed up, so yeah, I could have walked into it."

"Then why didn't you?" Patricia asked. "No one could fault you for that. Even if I would miss you. It's just the natural order of things."

Liz shrugged. "If the light had shone up before I got to know the Ravenswinds and Minehearts, I'd have gone willingly. Now? I kinda want to stick around for a while longer." She gave me a shy grin. "Could get interesting."

Oh, heck yeah, life around me was nothing if not interesting.

Whether that was a blessing or a curse was still up for debate.

I went back upstairs with every intention of sliding back into the nice warm bed beside my man. Only that's kind of hard to do when he's no longer there.

No, he was now sitting at the small table in the corner of the room reading something on his tablet.

"I take it we're up for the day?"

He grinned at me and motioned to all the boxes stacked up in the room. "Cardboard waits for no one."

I sighed. "Well, it can darn well wait for me to take a shower." I grabbed my housecoat from the chair by the bed and went in for a nice warm wake up. Five minutes later, I felt more than ready to take on the mass of cardboard awaiting our attention.

There's something to be said about almost meeting your maker. It tends to give you a real zest for life. Might as well put that zest to good use.

When I came out, Opie was still sitting there with his tablet.

"Please tell me whatever you're so interested in reading is good news and not bad. And if it's bad that, at the very least, it doesn't affect me or my family." I paused. "Or your dad, for that matter."

"Good news, actually, for once. I don't know if you'll remember this case or not, but it involved Jack Watson, so I'm betting you will. That bonsai garden that he stole? Well, it's back."

I walked over to stand behind him, and he took the hint and called up the article again on his tablet.

It was short, but he was right. It was very good news.

Celeste had gotten back her Bonsai baby, and Lily had offered an Olive branch.

Life was looking up again.

"Meow."

I glanced over at Destiny. She was sitting on the chair opposite Opie. When she saw she had my attention, she stood up and placed both paws on the folder laying on the table. I'd almost forgotten about it. The file that Patricia had dropped off with my council members to look into.

"Oh, come on. You were there last night. Can't I get just one day off?"

Her tail wagged and one pretty little calico paw tapped the file.

Opie laughed. "She's quite the little taskmaster, isn't she?"

I nodded.

Oh, he had no idea just how true his words were.

The End… for now. Stay tuned.

Did you know Belinda White has another series? If you are looking for another read in between the witches, check them out. They have werewolves—and more. Finders Weepers: Book 1 of the Benandanti Series.

A Note From Belinda

Thank you so much for reading Home Familiar Home. I truly hope you enjoyed it! Please check out my website at BelindaWrites.com for updates on upcoming books.

Also, if you can spare a few minutes, please consider giving my book a review. I'd really appreciate knowing what you thought of it.

The Gemstone Coven isn't nearly done yet. Amie and her crew will be back in a couple of months in book five of the series. I'm also hard at work on Opal's series. Hopefully that one will follow soon after Amie's is completed.

(And yes, I do hope to find the time to write the story of Opie's side adventure with his dad and Giovanni Rosati too. Could be a fun one!)

Lots to do. Better get back to it.

Belinda White
December 2019

www.ingramcontent.com/pod-product-compliance
Lightning Source LLC
Chambersburg PA
CBHW031038160726
47991CB00005B/1932